David's big, dark eyes were trained on her. For a moment, she stared right back. She felt her face get hot and her heart speed up. Wow, he was *really* cute. The moment stretched out until he blinked his long black eyelashes quickly, like he was trying to wake up from something, and stuck out his hand. Maddy's mind raced. Why exactly had she decided to skip that shower this morning? Wait, stop. Who cared if he was gorgeous? *You're not available, Madeline!* She summoned up an appropriately bored smile and she shook David's hand. His hand felt warm and firm against hers. She drew in her breath at his touch. What was going on? *Stop!* She took her hand away and awkwardly brushed some hair back from her forehead. Maybe she'd just had too much coffee . . .

Books by Hailey Abbott:

THE OTHER BOY

Hailey ABBOTT

HARPER TEEN
An Imprint of HarperCollins*Publishers*

HarperTeen is an imprint of HarperCollins Publishers.

alloyentertainment
Produced by Alloy Entertainment
151 West 26th Street, New York, NY 10001

Library of Congress catalog card number: 2007934551
ISBN 978-0-06-125383-6

Typography by Andrea C. Uva
❖
First Edition

Chapter One

◆

With the beat of a Gwen Stefani song pounding in her ears, Madeline Sinclaire clipped up her long blond hair and slid into the hot tub on her parents' deck. Steam rose up from the bubbling water, momentarily obscuring her friends' faces. She inhaled deeply and eased downward. Suddenly, something grabbed her feet under the water.

"Brian!" Maddy screamed.

Her boyfriend's sleek, wet head surfaced next to her, and everyone burst into laughter.

"What? Did I scare you?" Brian Kilburn asked, flashing his sexy little smile that curled just the edges of his mouth. After dating him for almost a year, Maddy still thought he was the cutest boy she'd ever seen. Brian's sleepy blue eyes could always melt her annoyance.

"Yes, you did, jerk!" Maddy said playfully. She punched him on his well-toned arm.

"Don't hurt him too badly," Morgan Gainsley called from the other side of the hot tub. "He's the only one left who knows how to tap a keg—Dave already passed out." She pointed to a dark shape lying in a heap on a lounge chair, barely visible through the San Francisco night.

"How is that possible?" Maddy giggled at her best friend. "The party just got started!"

"She's not going to hurt me," Brian growled. "Not before I . . ." He trailed off as he stood up in the water, grabbed Maddy, and tilted her back in his arms.

"Eeek!" She giggled, hoping she wasn't flashing the rest of the hot tub. Her D&G string bikini top didn't allow for a lot of gymnastics.

Brian went for her neck like a vampire. He started to run his mouth lower, but Maddy struggled upright and shoved him away.

"Okay, hornball. Save it for later," she said with a laugh.

Reluctantly, Brian released her and sat down again. Maddy settled back contentedly in the hot water, Brian's arm around her tanned shoulders. Light spilled over the deck from the open French doors behind her. The glow reached the manicured gardens at the edge of the two-acre lawn. Most of Richmond Country Day's upperclassmen, plastic cups of Miller High Life in hand, were packed into Maddy's living room, where the leather furniture had been pushed against the walls to make a dance floor.

On the deck, couples were cuddling on lounge chairs with beer bottles strewn on the ground next to them. Rob Davis had started a game of drunken tackle football on the lawn. "Touchdown!" a huge, hairy guy screamed as he grabbed the ball and landed headfirst in the shrubbery at the side of the yard.

Maddy smiled. Her first official house party of the summer was only an hour old, and she could already tell it was going be a great night. In fact, it was going to be a great *summer*–maybe the best ever.

Maddy's other best friend, Kirsten Owens, slid up next to her. "So when did your parents leave?" Kirsten asked, resting her elbows on the edge of the tub behind her, looking sleek and athletic in her navy blue Speedo. Maddy laughed. Even though Kirsten's idea of a relaxing Saturday was running a ten-mile race, Maddy still found it funny that she insisted on wearing a one-piece suit to a party full of bikinis and boys.

"This afternoon–*finally*," Maddy replied. "They should be arriving in Napa any minute now."

"I cannot believe you have the house to yourself for

two whole months!" Morgan squealed, splashing across the tub to join the other two girls.

"I know, right?" Maddy agreed. "You know, at first, they actually tried to tell me that I had to help them fix up that little midlife crisis—I mean, *vineyard*. But they couldn't resist my powers of persuasion—"

"And that A in AP English, you nerd," Brian teased.

She gave Brian a push. "Go get me another beer," she ordered playfully, admiring the muscles of his back as he climbed out of the hot tub and shook the water out of his dark hair. A tan line showed where the waist of his baggy navy trunks had dropped down a little. She heaved a sigh of delight as she thought of her and Brian—and her big, empty house—together, all summer.

"Girls, we're going to have so much fun!" she declared, stretching out her long legs and watching her toes bob in the bubbling water as her two best friends flanked her on either side. "First of all, we finally got to throw the party we've been planning since finals. And for the rest of the summer, we'll have shopping in Noe Valley, the beach every afternoon—"

"Parties at your place every weekend!" Morgan finished for her, sending a splash of steaming water toward each of the girls. "You have the best party house in San Francisco, Maddy."

"No question," Kirsten said, looking across the artfully lit pool to the view of the bay. Behind them the sprawling six-bedroom Spanish-style house pulsed with Rihanna's latest album.

Maddy smiled her agreement. Everyone was getting what they wanted: Mom and Dad were living their dream up in Napa, and *she* was experiencing sweet independence down here in the city.

"I should probably go mingle, guys," she told everyone. "I *am* the hostess, after all."

Brian splashed back into the tub next to her just in time to catch her last words. "Don't go too far," he said, winking at her meaningfully. Maddy laughed at him and pulled herself onto the deck, knowing he was enjoying watching the water run off her slim, tanned figure.

"If you tap that new keg, I might have a special treat for you later," she said flirtatiously.

He grinned back. "Wait, I want my party favor right now!" He grabbed for her, but she dodged his grasp and draped a silk sarong around her hips, slipping a gauzy linen shirt on top.

As Maddy made her way to the foyer, she saw Brian's best friend push through the oak front door. "Mad-e-line!" Chad yelled, crushing her with a bear hug. The hall filled up with huge, brawny boys lugging an extra case of beer. Two skinny blondes appeared behind them, each waving a bottle of vodka. Maddy shook her head—for two of the richest girls at school, Taylor and Sunny certainly managed to look remarkably cheap.

"We brought Grey Goose!" Sunny called.

"Your place is *so* awesome, Maddy!" Taylor squealed.

"Thanks," Maddy said. "Why don't you stick the vodka in the kitchen?"

"Oh my God, is that *Scott Winters*?" Sunny screeched in reply, staring into the living room. "Doesn't he play for UCLA?" She and Taylor hustled past Maddy, nearly knocking her over.

Within an hour, her house was filled with basically every person she knew—and a bunch she didn't. Maddy felt like the queen of summer. When she looked around again, Morgan and Kirsten were dramatically debating something with Taylor. Sunny was making out with a guy from Cathedral Prep. Someone had put on the Ying Yang Twins, and couples were grinding in the living room and making out on the sofas. Rob Davis broke a Lalique vase, and Maddy was drinking vodka tonics *way* too fast.

She needed a breather. So she made her way back onto the now-deserted deck, trying not to stumble too much. "Mmmm," she murmured, collapsing onto a canvas lounge chair. She closed her eyes and let the pounding music behind her wash through her mind. She could feel someone standing over her.

"I've come to collect my party favor now, hostess," Brian whispered as he slid onto the chair next to her. Maddy smiled and wrapped her arms around his neck.

He pulled her on top of him. "I am so glad your parents are gone."

"Me too." She loved the feeling of his whole body pressed against hers. She twined her fingers in the wavy hair at the back of his head and kissed him gently. His body tensed, and excitement shot through her. Mmm. Brian was so yummy. His lips always tasted like cinnamon.

He wrapped his arms around her and flipped himself over, taking her with him. Now he was on top, gazing down at her. "It's going to be a great summer, Madeline Sinclaire," he said softly as he pressed his hips against hers. She closed her eyes and he kissed her again, this time parting her lips with his tongue.

I couldn't agree more, she thought. She ran her hands up and down his bare back under his T-shirt as he shifted to the side a little and slid her shirt up. She shivered at the sensation of the fabric brushing her skin.

After a few blissful minutes, Maddy drew back and glanced at the diamond-encrusted Bulgari tank watch her parents had given her for her sixteenth birthday. Ten o'clock. By now, Mom and Dad would have unloaded all the wheelbarrows and pitchforks and whatever the hell they used to resuscitate a run-down vineyard and would be sipping wine, happily oblivious to the biggest party in Sea Cliff. "I should probably go make sure no one's throwing chairs out of windows or something," she said.

Brian groaned and reached for her.

"Don't leave yet."

She smiled and tried to pull him up. "Come with me!"

The packed living room was grinding to the heavy bass line. The crowd had spilled up the stairs—Maddy could hear some sort of thumping from her parents' room overhead—and into the kitchen.

"Rob, what are you doing in there?" Maddy called over to the brawny football player. Rob Davis had apparently given up on running around the yard and had just taken the top off of the blender.

"A little something I like to call Robbie's Late Night Bean Special," Rob answered with a grin. "You'll love it, Sinclaire."

The whir of the blender was just audible over the music. In the very back of her mind, Maddy briefly wondered if he was trashing the kitchen but decided it didn't matter. After all, she had two whole months to clean up, and right now, dancing to Beyoncé was her main priority. *Your love's got me looking so crazy right now.*

Brian's arm slid around her waist. He pulled her up tightly against him and handed her a cold beer from the freshly tapped keg. Maddy wrapped one arm around his shoulders, swaying her hips to the music, and took a sip with the other hand. "Mmmm," she murmured and buried her face in his neck. *Your touch got me looking so crazy right now.*

From behind her, she could hear Morgan shrieking, "Oh my God! She did not!" Somewhere, glass shattered. Maddy shook her hair back from her face and raised her arms in the air, swaying to the music. Brian took her chin in his hand and leaned down.

"You're the most beautiful girl I've ever seen," he murmured into her ear, his lips brushing the side of her face. Their eyes met as he slowly brought his mouth to hers.

Maddy felt like her whole body was electrified. She ran her hands down Brian's back as he dipped her backward.

"Ow! Ow! Go, Maddy!" Kirsten giggled, bumping her shoulder.

Maddy twirled around, her eyes closed, singing as loud as she could, *"Got me looking so crazy in love!"*

In the distance, she could hear someone calling her name. But the music drowned out the voice. She'd deal with it when this song ended. Beyoncé could not be ignored. Then the call came closer.

"Maddy! Madeline Sinclaire!"

That sounds like my father, she thought dreamily. *I wonder if they even have stereos in Napa.*

"MADELINE! SINCLAIRE!"

Wow, that really does sound like Dad. Maddy smiled to herself. But when she opened her eyes, her father was not smiling back.

Chapter Two

✦

Maddy froze. She could feel the blood draining from her face. Brian stumbled into her.

"Wha—" Then he looked up and went totally rigid.

All around her, the party was still going on. No one else had noticed her parents yet. Morgan stumbled out of the kitchen, a bottle of vodka in her hand. "Maddy!" she yelled. "Are there more glasses—oh, sh—Hi, Mr. and Mrs. Sinclaire," she said, quickly regaining her composure. "Happy Fourth of July. Isn't patriotism just the best part of being American?"

Neither of Maddy's parents had moved from the doorway. Her father's face was beet red and his eyes widened to cover about half of his face. As his body tensed, his head looked like it was sinking into the collar of his shirt. Her mother's face was completely white. "Morgan," she said in a strangled voice, "please turn off the music."

"Right. Right away!" Morgan bounded over to the stereo and cut Beyoncé off mid-cry. Everyone stopped dancing and looked around.

Quickly sizing up the situation, Chad cupped his hands around his mouth. "Busted!" he bellowed. *"Everybody run!"*

Pandemonium broke loose as people shoved out the back door, yelling, "Get out!" No one had the nerve to go past Maddy's parents, still standing in the living room doorway. Maddy's mouth was dry and the walls were spinning. Through her fog, she felt Morgan and Kirsten squeeze her hands as they ran toward the back door.

"Call me," Morgan managed to whisper.

And all of a sudden, everyone was gone. Only Maddy and Brian still stood together in the middle of the floor.

"Arrhmmm!" Bob Sinclaire cleared his throat pointedly.

Maddy winced. "You'd better go," she muttered to Brian. "I'll text you."

"Um, bye, Mr. and Mrs. Sinclaire," he tried weakly, giving Maddy a sympathetic glance. He awkwardly squeezed through the doorway.

Once the three of them were alone, Maddy's mother slowly walked into the room and sat down on the leather sofa. With a cry, she jumped back up, soaked from the pool of beer on the cushion. Her father's face was purple. Her mother gingerly perched on a sofa arm. Not looking at Maddy, she muttered, "We forgot the Vineyard Association paperwork."

Ah. Maddy righted an upturned chair and slowly sat down. She buried her face in her hands. She wasn't quite sure which was worse—the guilt she felt looking at her mother's face, or the regret that she was probably in the biggest trouble of her entire life. Her parents were silent, obviously waiting for an explanation—but really, what could she say? She should at least *try* to dig herself out of this, though. "Guys," she began, "I'm really sorry—"

"Sorry!" her father exploded. "What are you talking about? We leave this house for five hours, after spending a month going over the summer rules. All we want is to get a box of files and what do we find? A hundred drunken teenagers trashing our house!"

"Daddy—"

"And who is responsible for this? Who? Our daughter, who assured us that she would take care of everything this summer! 'Don't worry, Dad,' you said. 'I'll be just fine.' Well, this doesn't look like 'just fine' to me, Madeline!"

Maddy took a deep breath. "Look, Dad, just let me explain."

"Explain what, Maddy?" Mom said. Maddy's stomach sank all the way to her ballet flats. "This situation seems perfectly clear to me. We trusted you. You broke that trust."

Maddy had a horrible feeling she knew what was next. She desperately tried to head it off with a pitiful stream of babbling.

"I'm so sorry, guys! I promise, promise, promise it will never happen again—ever! It was going to be my only party, I swear, just a little reward after school, before senior year, to celebrate summer. I–I–" She searched around for something, *anything*, to appease them. "I won't even stay here this summer! I'll go live with Morgan—Mrs. Gainsley is incredibly strict."

"No," her dad said firmly. "You are going to spend the rest of the evening cleaning up this house, and then in the morning, you're going to Napa with us. So get started." The calmness in his voice sounded terrifyingly final.

Maddy let out her breath. "Okay, Dad," she said in a barely controlled voice. "I understand that I screwed up and that I should go to Napa for a while to help you guys out as my punishment. But how long are we talking about? A week?" She had to stop to control the tremor in her voice. "Two weeks? I'll help you clean and mow or whatever. . . ." She broke off. Both of her parents were staring at her.

"Maddy," Mom said.

"What?"

"Your father isn't talking about a short visit. You'll be helping out at the vineyard for the *rest of the summer.*"

Clunk. As silence fell over the room like a dead weight, Maddy's visions of the beach, Brian, and freedom floated out into the now-foggy San Francisco night. "The *entire summer.* . . ?" she croaked.

Her dad skewered her with a stare. He spoke as if Maddy were someone of severely limited intelligence. "Do . . . you . . . truly . . . think . . . you're . . . staying . . . here . . . after . . . all . . . this?" Maddy swallowed.

Debbie Sinclaire got up from the sofa and went into the kitchen. "This discussion is finished," she shot over her shoulder. There was a pause. Then an eruption. *"Madeline Sinclaire! Can you please explain why the* hell *there is bean dip all over this ceiling?"*

Maddy watched her dad stiffly walk onto the deck. He stood illuminated by tiki torches with his hands on his hips, staring at a lawn chair floating upside down in the pool. As Maddy stood to walk to the kitchen, she saw her father's shoulders slump as he slid his head into his hands. And she felt the best summer ever slip right through her fingers.

Chapter Three

✦

"O
w!" Weighed down by two huge duffel bags and dragging a giant suitcase behind her, Maddy stumbled as she stubbed her toe on the edge of the door frame. She managed to squeeze the bags through the door and wrangle them down the steps.

The morning was fresh and dewy, with puffy white clouds skating overhead in the deep azure sky, but it might as well have been sleeting as Maddy crammed her stuff into the trunk of the Lexus RX hybrid. *Good-bye beach, bye shopping, bye sleeping until noon, bye hanging out with Morgan and Kirsten. And mostly, bye Brian.* She had texted him that she was being kidnapped. *Rescue me!* she had typed, without much hope.

"Maddy! Did you remember your hiking boots?" her

mother's voice called from the house. The woman had no right to be this perky at seven a.m. "The terrain is pretty rocky up there!" Her mom sounded like she was relishing the thought.

"I did, Mom!" Maddy sang out through gritted teeth.

"Well, we're leaving in just a minute. Dad's just checking the air-conditioning one more time."

Suddenly, Maddy heard a car engine behind her. She whirled around to see Brian stepping down from his yellow Nissan XTerra.

"Hey, babe," Brian cooed. He was still wearing his clothes from the party, and his hair was all matted on one side, sticking up on the other. She could see sleep sand in the corner of one eye as he bent to kiss her forehead.

"You look awful," she noted. "Have you been home yet?"

He scrubbed at the side of his face with his hand. "No, I crashed on Chad's couch. I can't believe I'm awake this early. But I couldn't let you leave without saying good-bye." He leaned down to kiss her just as the front door slammed. Maddy clutched at Brian.

"Don't let them take me!" she whispered. "I am going to absolutely die up there."

He kissed her forehead again. "I'll call you every night." The garage door opened and Brian looked up. "I'd better go."

Maddy watched forlornly as he backed down the driveway and floored the accelerator. As he sped away, an arm appeared out of the driver's window and flapped a few times. She lifted her own hand in response and kept it up until the car had disappeared around the corner.

"Okay!" Mom came out of the house. She seemed to have recovered her good humor now that they were almost on their way back to Napa. "Got all your stuff in the car?" she asked Maddy.

"Yep."

Dad bustled up and slapped his hands together. "Everyone go to the bathroom?"

Oh. My. God. Was the entire summer going to be like this? She looked up at the sky, hoping to fight the overwhelming feeling that her world was shrinking beyond recognition. She climbed into the backseat and buckled her seat belt, planting her sneakered feet firmly on a box of dishes. "Let's just go already, okay?"

Her parents exchanged a classic our-teenage-daughter-is-such-a-pain-in-the-you-know-what glance. *Good*, Maddy thought. *We're all on the same page. I think you guys are a pain in the ass too*. She closed her eyes and leaned her head against the leather seat back. She could hear a double *bam-bam* as her parents got in and shut their doors. Maybe she could just sleep the whole way.

Peaceful silence filled the car as her dad wound through the streets full of Spanish-style and Victorian mansions and then bumped over the railroad tracks. He drove through a Hispanic neighborhood, where the bodegas and shops selling *quinceañera* dresses were crowded together with skinny brownstones. The brownstones gradually gave way to warehouses and car dealerships. They turned onto the highway. The soft hum of the engine and the comforting voices of NPR hosts filtered into the backseat. Maddy drifted away, her head lolling on her shoulder.

"Madeline." Her father's voice jerked her awake.

"Huh?" A trickle of drool had reached her chin. She wiped at it furiously.

Her mom twisted around to face the backseat. "Daddy and I want to talk to you about this summer."

Maddy groaned.

Her dad went on. "We're going to need you to pitch in and do some work on the vineyard grounds. You're starting at zero on the responsibility scale. This vineyard is very important to your mother and me, so we expect you to take this seriously."

"Umm?" Maddy tuned them out when her purse started buzzing. She slid her BlackBerry Curve out of her Kooba bag. CHAT REQUEST FROM MORGAN. She held it down by her side and pressed START CONVERSATION.

HOW R U?

AWFUL, OF COURSE—WHAT DO U EXPECT? Maddy typed without looking at the keys.

K AND I MISS U ALREADY! AT ORCHIDS 4 BRUNCH.

Maddy's stomach rumbled at the thought. Orchids had absolutely the best strawberry waffles in the city.

THANKS FOR THAT. I'M PROBABLY HEADING OFF TO EAT GRUEL ALL SUMMER.

GOING TO THE BEACH LATER—IT'LL BE SO WEIRD WITHOUT U.

I KNOW. ALL I WANT IS TO HANG OUT WITH YOU GUYS, SLEEP IN, AND SEE BRIAN. BUT I'M GOING TO BE SLAVE LABOR FOR THE NEXT TWO MONTHS.

POOR GIRL! MAYBE K & I CAN COME RESCUE YOU!

THAT WOULD BE SO GREAT. I DON'T THINK U COULD GET PAST THE PRISON GUARDS THO.

K & I WILL BE THINKING OF YOU. XOXO!!

Maddy pressed END CONVERSATION, heaved a gusty sigh, and stared out the window at miles and miles of pine trees; rocky, sandy soil; and distant, bluish hills. They passed a vegetable stand with a sign in the front that read TOMATOES $1/LB.

Of course, Maddy had seen pictures of Napa and its acres of twisty grapevines wrapping around the hills and spreading across the valley floor. But even though the vineyards were less than two hours from the city, Maddy had never actually seen one before. She leaned a little closer to the window. The land was completely covered in vines, stretching as far as she could see. Low stone walls lined the two-lane road. Hand-lettered signs reading WINE TASTING TODAY and NORTH RIDGE WINERY flashed by. Occasionally, they passed a palatial gate with the name of the vineyard spelled out in iron letters at the top. Past these gates were long, groomed gravel driveways lined with towering trees.

Maddy settled back into her seat, comfortably wiggling her shoulders into the cushy leather as she pictured a massive stone villa, surrounded by acres of manicured lawn. She'd be clad in a clingy black dress, pouring wine for a clutch of sophisticated vineyard visitors. "This is our newest blend, a merlot-burgundy," she imagined herself explaining. "It has very strong legs." Everyone nodded, impressed with her knowledge, and sipped delicately from their long-stemmed glasses. *Maybe this won't be so bad after all,* she thought as she dozed off.

Chapter Four

✦

H ere we are!" Her dad's voice was offensively cheerful.
Mom was rummaging around in her handbag, mut-
tering something about the keys.

Maddy leaned forward eagerly as the car turned onto
a long, rocky hillside. Twisted pine trees were around
them. She rolled down the window and inhaled a deep
breath of the fresh mountain air. It did smell good out
here.

The car slowed down and turned through an opening in a crooked wooden fence that looked about a hundred years old. An enthusiastic profusion of morning
glories and wisteria vines draped over the top rails.
Maddy squinted at a little wooden sign hanging
crookedly next to the driveway: IRONSTONE WINERY.

"Our front entrance," her dad announced grandly.

Maddy's vision of the lush vineyard with romantic stone buildings and polished tile floors began to crack.

Everyone hung on to their door handles as her dad swerved to avoid the gaping holes along the bumpy driveway. Maddy tried to focus on the looming pine trees surrounding them.

"Whoa!" Bob slammed on the brakes.

"Oh my God," Maddy said, squinting through the windshield from the backseat. "Is that a *pig*?"

Mom sighed. "Mr. Jenkins next door keeps them, and sometimes they get out. I believe that one is named Jasper." The enormous white pig meandered around the middle of the driveway. Bob blew the horn, which the pig haughtily ignored.

Mom opened her car door. "Let's see if he'll just walk off with a little urging. We can call Mr. Jenkins when we get to the house." Gingerly, she stepped toward the pig and put her hand in her pocket. She drew something out and flung it into the bushes by the side of the road. Jasper lifted his huge head, snorted, and lumbered off toward the object.

"What was that?" Maddy asked as Mom got back in the car.

"Oh, nothing." Her voice was airy. "I had some cheese crackers in my pocket."

"Wow. Now can we please drive up to the house?"

Maddy shook her head, trying to reconcile the sophisticated Mom she knew, who never left the house without her Chanel lipstick, with a woman who kept pig bait in her pocket.

Leaving Jasper happily eating his processed cheese, the SUV passed through the little grove and rounded one more turn. Maddy's father pulled up to a clearing in the grass. "Welcome to Ironstone Vineyard," he announced. "First tasting will be held in the wine room in"—he looked at his watch—"approximately two months."

Maddy stared at the structure in front of her. It was more a cottage than an actual house, and it looked like it belonged in an English fairy tale, not Northern California. Ivy covered the white clapboard sides, climbing to the slate roof. Curtains fluttered from the open windows upstairs, and a porch with elaborate wooden railings, scrolls, and gingerbread carving spread across the length of the house. The place was sitting in the middle of a giant, overgrown flower garden, where rosebushes competed with hollyhocks for the most sunshine. *Who lives here?* Maddy wondered. *Elves?*

Her parents practically leaped from the car as Maddy extracted herself from the backseat. The only sounds were of her parents rummaging around at the back of the car, the wind moving through the tops of the trees like the ocean hitting the shore, and a mockingbird singing madly on a branch over her head. The air was dry and cool in the shade, but when she stepped into the sunshine, she could feel its heat on her bare arms. She fished in her bag for her oversize Dior sunglasses. A mosquito whined in her ear. She swatted at it and slapped another one on her leg. Perfect.

"What do you think?" Mom picked up a big canvas bag and glanced at her daughter. Her father was busily pulling boxes and bags out of the trunk and piling them on the ground.

Maddy chose her words carefully. "It's . . . nice. Little."

Mom gave her an absentminded smile, but before Maddy could respond, she heard a crunching sound behind her. She turned to see a gray-haired man about her parents' age appear around the side of the house.

"Fred!" Her father waved the man over. "Maddy, this is Fred Tighe, our business partner."

"I'm glad to finally meet you, Maddy." Fred smiled at her through his beard, his eyes crinkling up at the corners. His voice was quiet and gentle as he wiped his hand on his canvas work pants and held it out. Maddy shook the outstretched paw.

"Nice to meet you, too," she said.

Fred turned to her father. "Bob, I want to take a look at the southwest irrigation ditch, if you have a moment. I know you all just arrived, but darned if that hose hasn't backed up and filled it in again."

"Damn. Not that thing again. You know, I think if we try that black tubing . . ." The two men disappeared around the side of the house, Bob gesturing and talking animatedly, Fred nodding.

Mom was loading herself up with bags and a big box of groceries. "The front door key is buried in my bag somewhere, but the kitchen door's open."

"Why can't we just pull the car around back?" Maddy asked. "That would be a lot easier than hauling all this stuff around."

"Grab that suitcase, will you? We can't pull the car around. The trees are too close—it won't fit."

"Mom, I have to pee so bad!"

"Well, go inside—take the suitcase with you. The bathroom's upstairs. There's only one."

"What?" Maddy couldn't hide her unintentional indignation.

Mom straightened up and pressed her lips together. She looked like she was about to say something but decided against it.

"Whatever!" Maddy said hastily. "What I meant was, great! I adore sharing a bathroom with my parents and assorted wildlife. Maybe Jasper the pig would like to move in also."

"Perhaps he would. Why don't you go back down the driveway and ask him?" Mom said calmly.

They heaved the bags and boxes around to the back,

which was covered by another shady porch. A swing and an array of wooden rocking chairs dotted the yard. Trellises stood against the sides of the house, covered in climbing roses. A large lawn spread out in a semicircle, surrounded on all sides by twisty grapevines. Clusters of lush purple grapes hung down. They looked delicious.

Ignoring her bladder, Maddy wandered over to the grapes and picked a few of the ripest. They were firm and smooth and covered with a hint of silvery frost. Her mouth was already watering. She popped them into her mouth and bit down. Hot, sweet juice spurted onto her tongue. Mmm. Wow. They were more intensely grape-y than anything she'd ever tasted. She glanced back at the house and carefully spat the thick skins and seeds onto the ground.

Maddy lugged her suitcase up the back steps and pushed open the screen door. She stepped into a little back hallway. She heard Mom already banging cabinet doors in a yellow-painted kitchen to her right. A steep wooden staircase extended up in front of her. She climbed the steps, listening to them creak under her feet. The upstairs hallway was narrow, with a few rooms visible through their half-open doors. Maddy briefly took in the cream-painted walls, wide-planked hardwood floors, and sunlight pouring in through open windows.

She spotted the bathroom at the end of the hall and darted in. It was tiny, with just enough room for a pedestal sink, a toilet, and a huge old tub that looked like it was made of copper. The floor was covered with old-fashioned black and white hexagonal tiles. A distressed old armoire painted shabby-chic white stood in a corner. Maddy thought longingly of the heated towel racks, three showerheads, and vast marble countertop of her private bathroom at home.

She turned on the water at the freestanding sink and stuck her hands underneath. *"Yowch!"* she yelped, and yanked her hands back, shaking off droplets of scalding water. Maddy glared at the sink. Two faucets. Of course this house would have a sink from like 1776 with separate faucets for hot and cold. She scowled and dried her hands on her sweatpants.

There were three other doors in the hallway besides the one leading to the bathroom. The first room had an antique rolltop desk pushed against a wall, an old sofa, and a bookcase overflowing with books and papers. A laptop sat on the desk. *That must be the room they're using as the vineyard office,* Maddy thought. She peeked into what must have been her parents' room next. A big bed with an old brass headboard stood in the middle of the room, surrounded by a sea of boxes. Every room had funny slanted walls and low wooden ceilings. Maddy felt like she was on a ship.

There was only one door left, at the end of the hallway. "Is this end room mine?" Maddy called down the stairs to her mom, who was still clattering around in the kitchen.

"Yes, it is!" she called back.

A cool breeze blew against Maddy's face as she walked in the door. Across the room, big glass doors leading to a balcony were flung open. The walls were a soft sage green. One wall slanted down almost to the floor. A little corner alcove held a built-in cushioned bench covered with pretty pillows. The polished wooden floors were bare except for a few woven rugs. A four-poster bed was covered with a green and white fern-patterned bedspread. There was a big, old-fashioned wardrobe in one corner and a white vanity table, the kind with a mirror on top, and a cushioned stool.

Maddie sat on the corner of the vanity table. What was she going to *do* here? Everything was so little and creaky and old. She felt caged in already. She stood and went over to the open doors. The green rows of grapevines stretched out for miles before her, with rolling grassy hills in the background, streaked here and there with bands of dark pine trees. Far away, on a hill, the tiny red dot of a tractor moved slowly across the landscape. Maddy couldn't help thinking of the view from her room back in the city, with the bay spread out like a wrinkled blue sheet, the Golden Gate Bridge shrouded in fog, and the city crowded to the edge of the water.

She reluctantly dragged the big blue suitcase into her new room from the hall. She felt exhausted, like she'd been traveling for a week. Just that morning, she had woken up in her own huge bed on silky Egyptian cotton sheets, snuggled up under her plush brown duvet in her room, with its remote-control lighting and sleek stereo system. But now she was sharing a room with eight million mosquitoes and Lord knew what other wildlife. And there was no escape.

Maddy gathered up an armful of dresses and skirts, most of them still on the hangers, and started stuffing them into the wardrobe in the corner. It took about thirty seconds for her to fill up the hanging section. She struggled to shove in a few more pieces, then stared first at the wardrobe and then at her suitcase in dismay. She hadn't unpacked even a quarter of the things she'd brought. Panting a little, she managed to shut the wardrobe door by hurling her shoulder against it. She stood back. The sleeve of a cashmere sweater was stuck between the door panels.

Maddy flopped onto the fluffy bedspread like a wet rag. "Ooohhh!" she moaned to the ceiling. "I am officially living my worst nightmare."

Chapter Five

❖

When Maddy's cell rang at dusk, she snatched it like it might magically transport her back to civilization and save her from morosely staring out at the gathering blue and purple shadows on the lawn.

"How's the prison inmate?" Morgan crackled from the other end.

"Oh my God! I am *so* glad you called!" Maddy cried, sitting up in her chair and lowering her feet from the porch railing.

"Hey, don't hold back or anything." Morgan laughed. "So, is it awful or what?"

Maddy stood and began pacing between the room and the porch, holding the phone in a death grip. "There was a *pig* in the driveway when we drove up!"

She yanked the phone away from her ear to dull the shrieks of her friend's raucous laughter. "Hey, you *could* be feeling sorry for me, you know," she said.

Morgan chokingly pulled herself together. "I know," she said weakly. "It's just that—come on. Madeline Sinclaire and a pig? Is he your new best buddy?"

"Very funny. And there's only one bathroom, all the rooms are tiny, and my hideous parents have already sentenced me to manual labor." Maddy flopped down on the bed and hung her head over the side. She stared at the rich brown floorboards and traced a little pattern with her index finger.

"Unbelievable. What's the deal with this place? I mean, why are they so obsessed with it?"

Maddy heaved a gusty sigh. "It's their *dream*," she said, rolling her eyes. "They've talked about buying a vineyard for practically as long as I can remember. The owners of this place went bankrupt because of some sort of insider trading scandal last winter. So they sold it really cheap and now my parents are convinced making wine is their destiny or something. And apparently *I* have to be part of it."

"Well, don't worry. They can't keep you up there for the whole summer, can they?"

Maddy laughed. "Why not? They can do anything they want." She knew Morgan was just trying to make her feel better, but she couldn't help her nasty mood.

"The party was hella fun, though," Morgan reminded her. "Everyone's saying it was the best one of the summer so far."

Maddy smiled. "Thanks, *chica*."

"And—"

Maddy sat up. "Wait, what's that noise?" A steady *cheep, cheep, cheep* was coming from one corner of the porch. She got up from the bed.

"What? Maddy, is it a bear?" Morgan cried. She sounded genuinely scared. Maddy went out onto the porch and peered into the dark corner. The cheeping stopped as if on a timer.

"No, Miss Hysteria, it's a cricket, not a bear. I'm not in the Yukon Territory." She backed away a step. *Cheep, cheep, cheep*. She moved forward. It stopped. Back. *Cheep*. Forward. Stop. "It's majorly annoying, though," she said as she retreated into her bedroom. The cheeping resumed, right on cue.

"Poor Mad—hey, I've got to go," Morgan said. "Kirsten's on the other line. We're all going to dinner in a few minutes."

"Who's going?" Maddy asked mournfully.

"Why are you torturing yourself? The usual: Brian, Chad, Taylor, Sunny, me, and Kirsten. Don't worry, we'll get an extra chair for you."

Maddy pushed her face into her pillow. "Thanks," she mumbled. "Bye."

"Bye. I'll call you."

Maddy tossed her phone onto the bedside table and lay staring at the darkness. *Cheep, cheep, cheep.* She sat up and turned the light on. The cheeping stopped. She turned the light off and lay back down. *CHEEP, CHEEP, CHEEP.* Maddy sat up again. "Shut up!" she yelled in the direction of the porch. The noise stopped for a moment, as if the cricket were considering its options, and then began again, deciding Maddy wasn't worth listening to. *Of course,* Maddy thought. *Because what I want doesn't matter anymore.*

Chapter Six

✦

"Maddy! Rise and shine, little bean!"

Maddy pulled the sheet over her head and rolled onto her stomach. "Mmmff," she moaned. She could hear someone coming up the stairs.

"'You are my sunshine, my only sunshine, you make me happy . . .'" Mom's voice grew louder as she entered the room.

Maddy lifted her head and clawed the sheet from her face. "Mom, *why* are you singing? What time is it?" She fell back into the comfortable embrace of her mattress and let her fingers graze the mosquito bites on her forehead. She had forgotten, of course, to close the doors to the porch last night.

"'You'll never know, dear, how much I love you, oh

please don't take my sunshine away!' It's six thirty, Sunshine." Mom was wearing one of Dad's button-down shirts with the sleeves rolled up and a pair of baggy khaki shorts. She strode over to the porch and leaned on the railing. "Ah! Just smell that Napa air! Isn't this porch darling? You could sleep out here if you wanted."

"Shhh," Maddy whispered, turning over on her side and fluffing her pillow. "Right now I'm sleeping in here. I'll be down in a few hours. Can you shut the door when you leave?"

"Get up, get up! Dad and I have already had break-fast. We have a whole plan for you, so be downstairs in fifteen minutes, my lovely." She left the door open behind her as she skipped out.

Maddy flopped onto her back and lay with her arm over her face. *Six thirty?* The woman was inhuman. And "a whole plan" sounded suspiciously like it might include large amounts of lifting and sweat. Grumbling, Maddy heaved herself out of bed and wrestled a short white cotton dress out of the bulging wardrobe. She briefly considered a shower, but realized that no one would see her except for her parents and Fred. She pictured Brian pulling up the driveway in his gleaming SUV, grinning at her from behind his Oakleys.

"Hey, babe!" he'd call out. "I came up to rescue you!"

Maddy shook her head to dispel the image. The

chance of Brian coming up to save her was about as high as the chance that her parents would actually let her spend another night alone in the next twenty years.

She pulled her hair up in a messy knot on top of her head and slipped her feet into a pair of Havaianas. Then she grabbed her huge sun hat from its nail on the wall and looked in the mirror. Ugh. Eyes puffy, face pale, so many mosquito bites that her forehead looked like the surface of Mars and . . . lo and behold, the start of a lovely zit smack in the middle of her chin. She ripped the hat off, tossed it on the bed, and stuck her sunglasses on her head instead. The last time she'd felt this gross was—actually, she'd never felt this gross.

In the sun-flooded kitchen, she sat down at the round wooden table and tried to stretch her eyes all the way open. Mom set an enormous spinach and cheese omelet down in front of her. Without even looking up, Maddy started devouring it, along with two pieces of sourdough toast.

"We've been having such fun eating local," her mother chattered as she bustled around the kitchen, putting away the omelet ingredients. "Those eggs are from our neighbors down the road. I found the goat cheese at a little grocery in town that sells all Napa-grown food. And the spinach is from our garden!"

"Great," Maddy mumbled with her mouth full. It was hard for her to muster up enthusiasm for the origins of eggs and spinach before seven o'clock in the morning. Debbie poured herself a glass of orange juice and sat down across the table.

"It's so relaxing out here," she went on. "The air gives me so much energy! Take a deep breath. Don't you just love it?"

"Um, yeah." Maddy was concentrating on heaping three teaspoons of sugar into her coffee. She needed the caffeine—immediately. Her head was pounding and her eyes refused to stay open without serious effort.

Mom jumped up as a truck engine rumbled outside in the front. "That must be Dad and Fred. They went down to talk about the harvest schedule with John Sands—our neighbor on the other side," she explained. "We might trade work to help each other out. Come on out when you're done, okay, honey?" Her voice trailed off as the screen door slammed behind her.

Maddy gulped her coffee in three swallows and immediately felt more awake. She lowered her sunglasses and clattered down the back steps. Under the pure blue Napa sky, the air was cool but held the promise of heat. The sun was shooting its lemon-yellow rays around the mountains and over the lush, green vineyard. In one corner of the yard, flowering quince glowed orange in the morning light. As she walked around to the front of the house, Maddy barely even noticed what a shack the place was.

"Hi, honey!" Dad called as he and Fred climbed down

from the cab of an ancient red pickup truck. "Come on over!" He handed his wife a bag of groceries, which she hoisted onto her hip and carted back around the house, giving Maddy a peck on her forehead as she passed.

"Morning, Fred! Morning, David!" Debbie called over her shoulder.

Maddy's head shot up. *David?* She peered over her dad's shoulder and finally noticed a guy with curly, sun-bleached brown hair sitting in the truck bed, his arms looped easily around his knees.

"Morning, Mrs. Sinclaire!" The mystery boy rose and vaulted over the edge of the truck, landing lightly on the ground. He stood about six feet tall, and his old, slim gray T-shirt hung easily from his broad shoulders and showed off the muscles of his chest and arms. Even from where she was standing, Maddy could see that his fore-arms were strong and corded, and he had the kind of tan that only comes from working outdoors.

"Maddy, I want you to meet David," her father said. "This is Fred's son. You two will be working together this summer."

What?

Somewhere in the background, her dad was still talk-ing. "Sorry, hon, I forgot to mention yesterday that David is staying up here at the vineyard for the summer too. Fred and I thought it would be great for you to work together."

David's big, dark eyes were trained on her. For a moment, she stared right back. She felt her face get hot and her heart speed up. Wow, he was *really* cute. The moment stretched out until he blinked his long black eyelashes quickly, like he was trying to wake up from something, and stuck out his hand.

"Hey, nice to meet you." His smile was wide and open and his teeth flashed white against the tan of his face.

Maddy's mind raced. Why exactly had she decided to skip that shower this morning? Wait, stop. Who cared if he was gorgeous? *You're not available, Madeline!* She summoned up an appropriately bored smile and shook David's hand. His hand felt warm and firm against hers. She drew in her breath at his touch. What was going on? *Stop!* She took her hand away and awkwardly brushed some hair back from her forehead. Maybe she'd had too much coffee. As Maddy considered switching to decaf, David casually stuck his hands in the pockets of his battered jeans and leaned against the side of the truck.

He smiled at her again. "So, you all got in yesterday, right?"

"Um, yeah." For some reason, she couldn't think of anything else to say.

David waited for a second and tried again. "Cool. What do you think of the place so far?"

"Obviously, it's great." The sarcasm was unintentional;

she was going for smooth. *Damn.* She felt like she was in school, standing at attention in front of him like she was about to recite the Pledge of Allegiance or something. She looked around for a place to sit, but there wasn't one, so she just crossed her arms awkwardly.

David seemed a little thrown. "Ah, yeah. The house is amazing. Have you seen the grapevines yet?"

She snorted a little, involuntarily. "Well, they're hard to miss." Arrrgg. *Mean* when she'd meant *friendly.* She was trying to be polite, but, honestly, this whole situation was just aggravating. The sun was too hot, her breakfast felt like a boulder in her stomach, and worst of all, she had *no* idea what "amazing project" her parents had cooked up for her and this guy. No matter how nice he was, he couldn't teleport her back to the city, and that was really the only thing she wanted.

David opened his mouth but then shut it abruptly and fixed Maddy with a quizzical stare, as if he was realizing something. "Yeah, I guess it's too bad if you're anti-grapevine. You're trapped by about three hundred miles of 'em," he said, rolling his eyes playfully and shooting her a rueful grin.

"Okay, kids!" Bob walked up, beaming. His bald head was sunburned, and he was already sweating in the strong mountain sun. He slapped his hands together. "Now, I have a really special project for the two of you."

Oh boy, Maddy thought. *Here it comes.* "What, Dad?"

"Well, I think I should just show you—it's going to be great when it's all done. Come on, let's take the truck." He climbed into the driver's seat of the red pickup.

"Um, Dad," Maddy asked, "where did you get this truck?" The windows were missing their glass, and the stuffing in the seats was bulging out everywhere. The inside of the cab was sprinkled liberally with dog hair and bits of straw.

"Got it at an auction when we came up here at Christmas. Remember, I told you about it?" Maddy did vaguely remember him going on about a great deal he had gotten up in Napa. "Climb in!"

David hoisted himself back into the truck bed. Maddy hesitated for a minute. She had never ridden in the back of a truck before. David was watching her from his perch on a straw bale.

"Want a hand?" he asked. He stood up and leaned over the edge, extending his arm toward her.

"No, thanks," she said, trying to sound airy. She perched her sunglasses on top of her head and climbed awkwardly onto the tailgate, trying to avoid flashing her hot pink bikini underwear. Her feet were sliding around—sneakers probably would have been a better choice. She was almost in the truck, when one flip-flop caught on something and slid off into the dirt. Maddy looked down in dismay. "Crap!" she said. She was caught in a very unflattering position—straddling the tailgate, one leg in the truck bed, one outside, with her rear sticking out, and clutching the edge with both hands. She swung a leg back over so she could hop down, but before she could, there was a soft thud behind her. In one motion, David reached down, tossed her the flip-flop, and effortlessly swung back into the truck.

"Thanks," she said, surprised.

"No problem." He winked at her. Maddy started a little. Damn, he was sexy. She settled herself on a bale of straw, and the truck engine started with a roar. She jumped at the noise before she could stop herself. David glanced over at her. She lightly tossed her hair and looked away. He leaned forward and raised his voice over the engine noise.

"Your dad seems unaware that there's this new invention called a muffler . . . ," he said, gesturing to the front of the cab. Maddy laughed in spite of herself, the wind blowing against her face and her hair flapping out behind her like a long golden banner.

The truck bumped over the rocky soil down a dirt track that wound between the rows and rows of vines. The grapes hung thick in their clusters beneath their canopies of green leaves. Despite the neat, curving rows, the place had a slightly wild air. Crows perched here and there, eyeing the grapes. A red-tailed hawk circled overhead, momentarily hanging in the air before folding its wings and silently hurtling toward the earth.

The truck stopped in front of a little stream. Maddy looked around at the rocky bank twisting along the field in a silvery streak until it disappeared out of sight between two hills. This must be the edge of the property. A broad meadow spread out on the other side of the stream, with tangled high grasses and scattered boulders competing for space with masses of blue and yellow wildflowers. The mountains lay brooding beyond, overlooking the landscape like sentinels.

Dad killed the engine, and David rose quickly and hopped out of the truck. Maddy followed cautiously, eyeing the distance from the bed to the ground, trying to calculate whether she could make it without losing any more of her clothing. She looked up, realizing that David was watching her again.

"Don't worry," he teased. "I won't look if you jump." Maddy scowled at him. The guy was reading her mind—it was uncanny. Irritating and uncanny. He came back up to the edge of the truck. "Hey, I was just kidding." He held his arms out. "Come on, I'll help you."

Maddy looked down into his sparkling, deep brown eyes from her perch in the truck, and awkwardly bent down, gathering the skirt of her dress between her knees. She grasped the edge of the tailgate with one hand and closed her fingers around David's with the other. She leaped down clumsily, almost falling. Quickly, he grabbed her around the waist. For a split second, his arms encircled her, hugging her against his broad chest. Maddy felt the warmth of his skin through his T-shirt and caught a whiff of fresh, piney soap and a vague scent like cedar chips. A tiny sigh escaped her. Flustered, she struggled upright. He quickly dropped his arms.

"Okay?" he asked, blushing a little.

"Yeah, fine," Maddy mumbled. She concentrated on brushing dust off her dress so she wouldn't have to look at him. Her knees felt a little wobbly, but she didn't know why. It wasn't like it was a big deal that he helped her down. She'd just tripped a little. This whole place had her off balance.

"Come on, you two!" Bob waved from the stoop of a small red wooden building perched on the stream bank. Dry yellow grasses lay in luxuriant swathes against the stone foundation, and the front entrance was draped in a profusion of wisteria. Maddy's dad pushed the oak door open, revealing an empty room beyond. Maddy and David stepped inside.

The space was square, with bare plaster walls and a plank floor. There was no ceiling, only the underside of the roof and rafters soaring twenty feet overhead. Swallows swooped in and out of an open window set high into the wall. Sunlight filtered through the wavy old glass of the windows and painted shadow patterns on the floor. A faint film of dust covered everything.

"The last owners used this for storage," Bob explained.

"But it was originally a barn for goats, back when this was a farm as well as a vineyard. You can see how solidly it's built."

"Yeah, it really is," David said approvingly, knocking on the wall. Maddy gazed longingly out the window, wishing that she could see San Francisco from here. She whipped her head around and saw that both Dad and David were staring at her.

"Mmmhmm!" she managed, pretending to admire the cobwebby walls. "So, what's the plan, Dad?" *Might as well get it over with.*

"Well! Glad you asked!" Her father grinned like a little boy. "You can see that the structure is in good shape. All it needs is a quick scrubdown and then . . . Fred and I want you two to transform it into our new wine-tasting room!" He paused for their reaction. David lifted his eyebrows slightly.

"Ah . . . great, Bob," he offered.

Maddy's father barreled ahead. "We want you two to take complete charge of this project, planning what you want in the room, ordering glasses, tables, chairs, wall art, rugs—after it's cleaned up, of course."

Maddy couldn't help herself. "So, this is where the vineyard visitors come to get trashed, right?" She widened her eyes innocently.

"Very funny, Madeline." Her dad looked annoyed. "The tasting room is where the visitors *taste* our wines—

explore their nuances, discuss their various qualities. They can go into town if they want to drink themselves silly. This is supposed to be a refined, relaxing room where people can focus on tasting good wine, enjoying conversation, and . . ." He strode over to the opposite side of the shed, where huge sliding doors stretched the entire length of one wall. Puffing a little, he pushed one back. Sunlight immediately flooded the room as he pushed open the other door. "Feasting on the view!" he finished triumphantly.

Maddy gazed out on the stunning view of the mountain. There was slightly awed silence as everyone took it in. Then David piped up. "Amazing. This is going to be great. Right, Maddy?"

All she could do was stare at him in dismay. What had happened to her summer? Tanning? Partying? Sleeping late? What was she doing here, in a former goat barn in the middle of the country?

Her father, however, seemed oblivious to the intense pain he was causing his only child. "Well, Fred and I are going to lay irrigation hose in the far quadrant today. I've got some cleaning supplies—buckets, rags, and a couple of mops. There's water outside." He pointed out the window, where Maddy could see an old-fashioned metal spigot standing in the middle of a bare patch of ground. "Take some time to look around. And then get started."

Maddy stared pleadingly at her father, but he didn't seem to notice. She was stuck. Her dad waved over his shoulder as he left.

David turned and walked over to a pile of cleaning stuff in the corner. His footsteps mixed with the noise of the stream burbling outside in the quiet of the shed. Maddy sighed as she sat down on an upturned bucket. She bent over and inspected the pedicure she'd gotten the day before the party. Chipped. And her bucket chair was filthy. She jumped up and twisted around. Great. She tried, fruitlessly, to brush off the giant dust mark on her skirt with her hands. She looked up and saw David staring at her. "What?" she snapped.

His eyes widened in surprise. "So . . . ," he started, "what's the story with you?"

Maddy rolled her eyes. "What story?"

He sat down on another bucket and laced his fingers together. She heard his spine crack as he stretched his arms over his head. "What's your deal, Madeline Sinclaire? I mean, why are you here?"

She walked away and looked out the window. "I have no idea, but I plan on leaving as soon as I possibly can." She didn't plan on telling this guy the story of her party disaster. Why bother?

There was a pause. "Well, why don't you leave now? What's stopping you? It's pretty obvious that you're not happy here."

Maddy snorted audibly. "You've got that right. And leaving isn't an option. I wouldn't be here if my parents weren't forcing me to stay." She turned around and studied him. "So, this is a pretty exciting summer for you, huh?" she asked defensively. "Playing in the dirt for two months?"

He shrugged. "Actually, I had an awesome summer job lined up, but my dad asked me to come up and help him instead. I don't mind—the food's better up here."

"Oh, yeah? What job was that, herding sheep?" She knew she was being incredibly bitchy, but David was starting to irritate her as much as the one stupid, tiny bathroom. He obviously loved it here, which was just about the weirdest thing ever. What normal seventeen-year-old actually *liked* being stuck on a farm all summer?

"I was going to clear trails at Sequoia National Park with my buddy," he explained. "We worked there last year too. It was awesome."

"Oh." Maddy had nothing to say to that. She sat down again and took out her BlackBerry to see if anyone had called to say they missed her.

David shrugged his shoulders and strolled back to the corner with the supplies. He rummaged around for a second and cleared his throat.

"What?" Maddy looked up from her BlackBerry. No messages. Not a single e-mail.

"Well, nothing, really. It's just that your dad forgot to

give us any soap or bleach or anything. It's just buckets and rags and mops."

"Oh, okay." Maddy was happy to hear it. Maybe they could just skip cleaning.

David tilted his head to the side as he spoke. "So . . . we should get some," he said slowly, as if speaking to a child.

Damn it. Thanks a lot, Napa Boy. She sighed through her nose. "Um, maybe there's some at the house?"

David considered this. "I have a better idea," he said, grabbing a broom and knocking some dust off one of the windows. "Why don't you go down to the grocery store on 17? Mitchell's. They'll have everything we need." He continued sweeping the window, watching her.

She leaped from her perch on the bucket and stuck her BlackBerry in her pocket. Saved from cleaning hell! "Okay. No problem," she replied. "What do we need? A bottle of bleach and some Mr. Clean? I'll be back soon!" She was out the door and halfway up the path before he could reply. The fresh mountain air against her face and the sun reflecting off the glossy grape leaves were as enticing as the thought of escaping the vineyard—even if it was just for an hour. Sweet freedom!

Chapter Seven

✦

When she got to the house, Maddy rushed into the front hall. "Hello?" she called. Silence. Everyone was out working. Perfect. She searched through the seed catalogs, pieces of twine, and old junk mail covering the hall table for the keys to the Lexus. All she found was a single key attached to a dirty leather fob. It looked suspiciously like . . . Maddy ran to the front porch. The only vehicle in the driveway was, unfortunately, the red pickup truck. *Crap. Dad must have ridden with Fred.* She eyed the key and then stared at the truck. What the hell. She *had* to get out of here.

Maddy clattered down the wooden porch steps and wrenched open the heavy driver's-side door. She hesitated briefly at the sight of the ripped gray cloth seat with its exposed stuffing. Then she shrugged, climbed onto the running board, and hoisted herself into the driver's seat, where she took a deep breath and brushed her hair back from her sweaty forehead. The interior reeked of dog, mildew, and something else—something familiar and disgusting. Maddy sniffed once and again, resisting the urge to put her hand over her nose. She craned around. There, stacked in the truck bed, was the source of the disgusting odor: four big bags of fertilizer, also known as horseshit. Delightful.

Maddy faced front again and cranked the key in the ignition. She jumped as the engine roared. It was like sitting on a dragon. She threw the car into drive after a brief struggle with the sticky old gearshift and carefully turned around in the driveway. She scraped against a few branches as she pulled out. *This isn't too bad,* she thought. She remembered to signal and turned onto the main road, firing the truck up to thirty-five. It shuddered a little but obeyed. *Woo-hoo. Now we're rocking.* The road unfurled before her like a ribbon and the breeze whipped in at her. Maddy sighed happily and reached her free arm out the window to feel the sun.

She had just passed a makeshift billboard reading MITCHELL'S GROCERY FOR ALL YOUR NAPA VALLEY NEEDS! 2 MI. in splashy red letters when her BlackBerry buzzed on the seat beside her. She picked it up and glanced at the screen. It was Brian. Finally! She pressed ANSWER.

"I am *so* glad to hear your voice!" she squealed.

"Hey, babe," he replied. Brian sounded like he was talking from the bottom of the ocean. Keeping one eye on the road, she looked back down at the screen. Only one bar.

"Brian, the connection is terrible. I'm in the car."

"What? I can't hear you. Go somewhere else."

"I can't! I'm *driving right now*!" Great. Four words into the conversation and she was already snapping at him.

"Okay! I can hear you now! Why are you yelling at me?"

She sighed. "Sorry. I'm in the worst mood."

"Well, I was going to ask how it's going up there, but I guess I don't have to."

"It completely sucks. I have to fix up a shed. I'm supposed to be cleaning it right now, but I escaped."

"Do you want me to drive up and rescue you?"

"Yes! But you can't. The party is still too fresh in my parents' minds. . . ." She was getting a crick in her neck from attempting to cradle the BlackBerry on her shoulder.

"I'm going to L.A. tomorrow anyway. But you know, I was thinking about your birthday next month. They'll have forgotten about the party by then. Why don't you get them to let you come back here for the weekend?"

"Are you kidding? I'm surprised they don't have me in chains. I think they're worried I might run away or something if they let me off the property."

"Tell them you'll stay at Kirsten's."

"I don't know," Maddy said doubtfully. "Maybe. I have to soften them up a little first." She was vaguely aware that she was passing the grocery store, a big white building with a red sign on her right, but she kept driving.

"I really miss you." Brian's voice was soft.

Maddy felt tears creeping into her eyes. "I miss you too. Call me every day!"

"Well, I told you I'm going to L.A. But I'll call you when I can. Just forget about all that work for a while. You need to take a break and chill. You sound awful. Why don't you go do something fun?"

"Maybe I will." She sniffled. "Bye." She dropped her phone onto the passenger seat and took a deep breath. Brian was right. Buying bleach wasn't going to improve her mood. Maddy drove past pastures of dry yellow grass with black-and-white cows lying in clumps on the hillsides, interspersed with little wooden cottages. The occasional irrigation pond sparkled blue under the cloudless sky. She snorted to herself. Who was she kidding? What was she going to do around here for fun? Go swimming with the cows?

The road widened as she approached a little town. Maddy eyed a small group of buildings clustered next to the street, shaded by massive redwood trees. Maybe there would be a coffee shop or something—*wait!* She jammed on the brakes, pitching herself against the seat belt. Glancing in the rearview mirror for confirmation, she read an elegant yellow and black sign out loud: "Oasis Day Spa."

She glanced around quickly and reversed the truck right back to the entrance. She killed the engine and quickly glanced at herself in the mirror, which was held together mostly with duct tape. Mmm. Hair wild and dry, dark circles under her eyes, skin flaking and red. It was a crime for her to walk around looking like this. *Right,* she thought. *No one should have to see me in this condition.* It was only right that she stop and have a couple treatments done. She'd be doing the people of Napa a public service.

Maddy climbed down from the ridiculously high cab and did her best to brush off the assorted bits of straw, seat stuffing, and dog hair that were clinging to her dress. She gave up and marched through the tinted glass front doors of the spa. *Ahh,* she thought as she entered. *Sanctuary.*

The lighting was soft and dim, and Maddy could hear soft harp music in the background. A fountain in the corner tinkled soothingly. The air smelled like lavender and clean towels. Maddy wanted to kiss the carpet, but instead she addressed the dark-haired young woman behind the desk. "Do you have any open appointments today?"

The girl smiled as if she knew everything Maddy had been going through. "You're in luck. We just had an entire wedding party cancel for the afternoon. The bride had an allergic reaction to a kiwifruit and swelled up like a bullfrog," she said cheerfully. She handed over the menu of treatments. "Can I recommend the Seaweed Stress Service? If you don't mind my saying so, you kind of look like you could use it."

Maddy touched the scaly skin on her cheeks and heaved a huge sigh. "I don't mind at all. Actually, I couldn't agree more. I'll take the seaweed treatment and a hand and foot massage, too."

Fifteen minutes later, Maddy found herself reclining on a cushioned table in another dimly lit room, listening to a nature sounds CD, while a girl named Tamara slathered her bare skin with a warm seaweed mixture the color and consistency of canned spinach. *Bliss. Utter bliss.* Tamara pressed a cold cucumber pack over Maddy's eyes and began kneading the bottoms of her feet. She quickly forgot all about bleach and cobwebs and annoyingly cute Napa boys as she drifted off into a delicious vision of her, Brian, a sailboat, and a freshly popped bottle of champagne. . . .

Chapter Eight

✦

"Maddy." Mom's voice came through the door of Maddy's room.

"Wha—?" She drowsily opened her eyes. Her seaweed wrap and massage had so completely relaxed her that after leaving the spa, she'd come straight back to the house (without any Mr. Clean), sneaked upstairs, and promptly fallen asleep. There were now shadows gathering in the corners of the room. She had even managed to ignore the cricket, who was still cheeping away in his corner of the porch. The door opened. "Mmm—what time is it? I fell asleep."

Mom sat down on the side of the bed. "I can see that." She smoothed Maddy's hair gently. Maddy closed her eyes again. Mom's soft hand felt nice on her forehead.

"Don't go back to sleep, honey. We forgot to tell you that we're having guests for dinner tonight. We're going to eat out on the lawn."

"Okay. Who's coming?" Maddy mumbled.

"Well, I bet you didn't know we had a famous chef living right down the road, did you? His name is Anthony Shepard and he has a wonderful restaurant in Rutherford. And he asked if he could bring his daughter tonight. She just arrived in town for the summer also— I think she's about your age. And there will be us, and Fred and David, of course."

Maddy opened her eyes. "Fred and David?"

"Well, naturally. This will give you a chance to get to know everyone better. Did you have a good time working with David today?"

Maddy turned and faced the wall. "It was okay." If she was going to ask about her birthday, now probably wasn't the time to tell Mom that she hated cleaning, hated being stuck in that shack, and had blown off her work for a spa day.

"Oh, good, honey. But you need to get ready, because we're eating at nine, and it's eight already. And I found a little something for you when I went to town for groceries this afternoon. Just look at this darling dress I found at a little boutique called Sun and Moon." She rummaged around in a shopping bag by her feet and came out with a coral red silk strapless dress. Maddy couldn't believe it—it was adorable. Usually Mom tried to get Maddy to wear "classic" outfits—which, translated, meant stiff collars and prim buttons.

"That's so cute! Thanks, Mom."

Her mom smiled. "I can't believe you like it. This may be a first for us." Maddy grinned back as Mom rose from the bed. "Oh, by the way, honey, when you take your shower, remember, the hot and cold faucets are reversed. You have to turn the cold all the way on first and then off, *then* turn the hot on, and then turn the cold back on. And don't worry if the pipes scream a little." She must have noticed the stricken look on her daughter's face, because she gave Maddy a reassuring little pat on the knee before leaving.

After her shower in the tiny bathroom, during which Maddy just barely managed to remember the instructions for hot and cold, she combed her hair in front of the vanity mirror in her room. She turned and gazed out the porch doors at the fading sunset. A crimson line burned just above the black silhouette of the mountains. Above the scarlet, the sky had melted into its deepest shade of blue. She could just make out the evening's first tiny star.

She felt as if the gathering dusk had smoothed her afternoon's rough edges. Her face was still glowing from her shower, and a touch of sunburn tinged the bridge of her nose and the tops of her cheeks. Her shoulders shone smooth and brown as she zipped up the red pleated dress. It fit perfectly. The patterned silk slid against her skin and fluttered just above her knees. She decided to skip the jewelry and tucked her long hair behind her ears, letting it hang over her shoulders. Barefoot, she headed down the stairs to the kitchen, where Mom was pulling a giant rack of lamb studded with rosemary out of the oven. "Mmm! That smells great!"

"Remember Mr. Jenkins who owns Jasper the pig? He brought over the lamb this morning. He feels bad that Jasper got out again."

"Oh. That was nice of him, I guess." Apparently, in Napa, people apologized with animal parts. "What else are we having?"

"Will you get the corn salad and bring it out back? We're going to eat at the picnic table." Mom's face was flushed as she carved the lamb. She glanced at the clock. "Uh, we're having cold cucumber soup and the tomato-corn salad, and Anthony brought a chocolate-almond torte for dessert."

"Yum." Maddy loved cold cucumber soup. She hefted the big white bowl and balanced it on one arm as she stuck a wooden serving spoon in it. The screen door banged behind her and she stepped onto the back porch. The yard was dark, save for the flaring candles on the picnic table and some light spilling from the kitchen windows. After her eyes adjusted, she could see a little knot of people standing on the lawn with drinks in hand. She could see David's rangy figure slouching off to one side. Everyone turned at the sound of the screen door.

"Maddy!" Her father waved. "Come and meet Anthony and Rain!"

Anthony and who? She hugged the heavy salad bowl as the cool grass slipped between her bare toes. She felt a little self-conscious with everyone watching as she approached.

Bob announced, "This is my lovely daughter, Maddy." He gave her a little one-armed squeeze.

Fred smiled at her. David faked a look of surprise. "Wow! You're here! I thought maybe you'd been kidnapped by grocery baggers or something," he said, pressing his hand to his chest. "I was so worried."

Maddy ignored him. "Hello," she said to the tall, skinny man standing next to her father. He had longish black hair that hung in his eyes.

"Hello," he replied quickly, his eyes darting somewhere over her shoulder.

"And this is Rain," Maddy's father went on.

"Hi," the girl said casually. She was tall and lanky, with tan arms and sun-streaked light brown hair that hung over her shoulders in wind-tousled strands. She was wearing worn jeans and a white tank top with a couple of string bracelets looped around one wrist. She looked like a surfer or maybe a lifeguard. Maddy wished she hadn't chosen the silk dress. It seemed fussy all of a sudden.

"Maddy!" her mother's voice called from the house.

"Oh, sorry," Maddy said. "I think I'd better—"

"Go help your mom," her dad said. "I was just going to show everyone the aging room before we eat."

The group trailed away across the grass. Anthony, Fred, and Bob talked animatedly in the front, with David and Rain side by side at the back. Their tall, lean figures matched somehow. *They could pass for brother and sister,* Maddy thought.

She forced herself to stop staring and went over to the long trestle table at the very edge of the lawn, where the grass ended and the grapevines began. She placed the salad bowl at one end and stepped back to admire the surprisingly romantic setting. The table looked gorgeous. Maddy's mother had used cream-colored linens and scattered flickering candles every-where. The air was redolent with the scent of the big bunches of lavender arranged in ceramic vases at either end. Maddy couldn't help tilting her head up, her mouth open like that of a little kid, and gazing at the stars flung like powder across the black velvet sky. The night sky always had sort of an orange cast from the city lights reflecting off the clouds in San Francisco. It never got this purely dark.

Maddy's mom came up next to her, balancing the giant platter of lamb. Fragrant steam curled up from the hot, pink meat. "Isn't it just lovely out here?" she said, moving some of the candles around to make a place for the platter.

"Yeah," Maddy admitted. "I've never seen so many stars before."

"I thought the same thing the first time Dad and I came up here." Across the yard, Maddy could see the shadowy forms of the group returning from their tour.

"Oh my goodness, this looks wonderful, just wonderful," Anthony said, flitting around the table like an excited child.

"Well, we're ready to eat. Have a seat," Mom waved her hands over the table. Everyone shuffled around, pulling out chairs and shaking out their napkins.

For a few minutes, the only sounds were of the clink of silverware and the rustle of the breeze in the vines just behind them as people concentrated on their food. David sat next to Maddy, and Rain sat across the table.

"Debbie," Anthony said, putting down his fork for a moment, "this is all wonderful—wonderful! I'll take some more of the corn salad."

"Here, just pass me your plate." Maddy's mom smiled as she dished out a generous portion of salad.

Fred and Bob were discussing oak versus metal

fermenting tanks at one end of the table. David glanced over at Maddy. "Always business," he said with a grin.

Rain turned to David. "So, I know this sounds weird, but you look really familiar. Did you go to Redwood Lake Camp?"

"Yeah, I did," David replied, scooping up a forkful of corn salad. "I was actually thinking the same thing about you. I went there for years, and then I was a counselor the summer before last."

"Wait—me too!" Rain laughed. "That must be what I was thinking of."

Maddy concentrated on her plate. Perfect. Now she had to listen to these two bond? And how did that girl get her arms so toned? She looked around the table. Every face was relaxed and smiling in the soft candle-light as people ate and drank and chatted. She was the only one who wasn't having a good time and, apparently, the only person on the planet who didn't *love, love, love* Napa Valley. Maddy stuffed a bite of lamb into her mouth and chewed morosely.

Next to her, David and Rain were still falling all over each other in the ecstasy of their shared memories of Camp Oak Tree or whatever it was called.

"Remember that girl Miriam, the drama counselor?" David was saying. "I ran into her out in Colorado. She's dating that Israeli guy—what was his name?"

"Itai! Oh my God, I haven't thought about him in forever!" Rain laughed.

"Hey, do you remember that one canoe trip . . ." David dropped his voice. Rain erupted into giggles, putting her hands over her mouth.

Maddy's face was growing hot and she could feel her jaw clenching. It was actually really rude of them to be telling inside jokes right here at the table, she thought, twisting her napkin in her lap. Not that she cared, because she didn't. But you'd think that if they wanted to have a freaking Camp Firewood orgy, they'd do it somewhere else.

Rain must have sensed something, because she abruptly broke off her conversation with David and leaned toward Maddy. "So, when did you get here?" she asked.

"Hmm?" Maddy pretended she hadn't heard at first. "What? Oh, yesterday." She offered a tight smile. There was an awkward little pause.

Then Rain nodded. "Yeah, I just got in this morning." More silence.

Maddy felt like she should at least attempt conversation, even though this girl totally didn't deserve it. "So, what are you up to this summer?" She tried to sound friendly.

"I'm working for my aunt. She has a stable up here. I'm leading trail rides for the tourists, mostly."

"Oh, wow." Maddy nodded sympathetically. "I had to work at the country club pool one summer. I hated it."

Rain looked confused. "That's . . . too bad. But, um, my job is actually incredible. I love riding and, this way, I get to do it every day."

"Oh, yeah. Of course." Maddy pretended to pick up her napkin to cover her embarrassment. How was she supposed to know leading trail rides was a great job?

"That's cool," David chimed in. "I've only been riding once or twice, but it was so fun. Do you guys get to gallop and things?"

Maddy was quiet for the rest of the meal. All around her, the conversation flowed effortlessly, like water around a stone. Why should she bother being sociable when everyone was doing just fine without her help? She didn't even have an appetite for the chocolate-almond torte, although she had to admit that it looked incredible. She just gazed at the vines, letting the breeze and the moonlight reflecting off the glossy grape leaves soothe her.

Eventually, Bob pushed back his chair. "Anyone up for a moonlight stroll?" he asked. "I think we could all use a little exercise after that wonderful meal." He looked over at his wife.

"You all go ahead," she said. "I'll just clean up a little." The group rose from the table slowly and gathered wraps and wineglasses. Debbie started stacking plates.

"I'll help you clean up, Mom," Maddy volunteered. Her mother looked up, a little startled.

"Don't you want to—?"

"No. I want to help you." There was no way she wanted to spend one more minute with these people. Besides, if she could get her mom alone, it would be the perfect chance to ask about her birthday.

"Okay, honey. Let's get all the dishes in first."

Maddy gathered up the used silverware and dumped it into an empty serving dish. Then she made her way across the cool, dark grass toward the warm glow of the kitchen.

Inside, Debbie started filling the sink with soapy water for the dishes. Maddy wrapped up some leftover cake. "Well, I think that went well," Mom chattered, splashing around with the sponge. "I love that corn salad recipe, but what do you think about white corn, Maddy?"

"Mom," Maddy interrupted. Her mother stopped talking and looked over. Maddy took a deep breath. She would have to approach this carefully. "You know, my birthday's next month. . . ."

"I think I just might remember that." Maddy's mom gave her a little smile as she scraped cucumber scraps into the compost bucket.

Maddy took a deep breath. "I was thinking that maybe I could go down to the city just for that weekend, to celebrate." Her mom's back tensed, but Maddy rushed ahead. "I could stay with Kirsten—"

"We'll see," Maddy's mother cut her off. "Let's see how it goes here before we talk about any privileges."

Maddy's plan was teetering on a very dangerous ledge. "I know, but I was thinking that if I stayed . . ."

"I heard that part. I also heard you tell Dad and me that you would be completely responsible if we left you alone all summer. And I seem to remember seeing patio furniture floating in my swimming pool and a roomful of underage teenagers spilling beer on my leather sofa. Let me talk to your father."

Bam. The plan fell to the floor and shattered into a million pieces. Her dad would never let her go. Maddy's mother heaved the big roasting pan into the soapy water. "Would you go out to the porch?" she said, raising her voice over the sound of the taps. "I think there are still some empty glasses out there—everyone was sitting out front before dinner."

Maddy nodded and trailed slowly through the darkened living room and foyer out to the front door. She struggled to contain her disappointment. She'd known any chance of celebrating her birthday in San Fran was iffy, but there was always a *chance*. Maybe she should have waited longer. That was it—she'd just ask later, after they saw that she'd been on her best behavior.

The front porch was unlit, but as her eyes adjusted,

she could see well enough to gather the scattered wine-glasses onto a tray. She padded down the porch steps and had just rounded the side of the house when she heard someone talking. It sounded like the voice was coming from the front, where she had just been. She stopped, listened, and realized the voice was David's. He must have just come back from the stroll through the vines and hadn't noticed her in the dark on the porch. He was talking to someone standing in the yard, near the parked truck. The cicadas and crickets were making a giant racket in the trees, but when she held her breath, she could make out his words.

". . . stuck here the whole summer," he was saying.

"Well, I don't know what you guys are going to talk about all day. You're really different." Maddy inhaled sharply. He was talking about *her*—and with that bitchy Rain!

"I don't know—my mom always said I could talk to a potato if I had to. I mean, come on. We can talk about . . ." David trailed off.

Maddy cringed as Rain laughed. "See? You can't think of anything. You might as well just face it—she's a spoiled suburban brat. I mean, she practically gagged at dinner when I told her what I was doing this summer."

I did not, Maddy thought.

David laughed a little. "She's definitely nothing like I expected she'd be, that's for sure."

Maddy had had enough. She couldn't believe they would talk about her this way. As she backed away, her toe caught the edge of a wicker rocker and sent her stumbling forward, almost off the porch steps. *Crash!* The tray fell, shattering the glasses all over the porch. David stopped talking. Overwhelming silence was broken only by the constant cheeping of the crickets. Maddy stood rooted in place. Slowly, David's figure turned and peered up at the porch. As soon as he saw Maddy, his eyes went wide. He opened his mouth as if to speak, but Maddy shot him her most scornful glare and turned her back, walking into the house with slow deliberation. She could feel his eyes burning into her back until the door shut behind her with a bang.

Forgetting about the mess of broken glass, Maddy tore up the stairs to her room and slammed the door. Her heart pounded under her ribs, and her breath whistled through her nose with anger. With fists clenched, Maddy threw herself onto the bed and stared up at the ceiling, where a small spider was peacefully spinning a web in one corner. Everything was quiet and then . . . *cheep, cheep, cheep!*

"Shut up!" Maddy shouted, and bolted from the bed. Furiously, she yanked open the porch doors. The cheeping stopped. Silence again. She stood still for a second and then turned and slowly went back into the room. She laid down and reached for her BlackBerry to call

Kirsten. *CHEEP, CHEEP! CHEEP, CHEEP!* It was never-ending. Maddy threw the phone on the bedside table and rolled over, pulling a pillow over her head. Forget it. Why was everything going wrong? She had never felt so out of place. No wonder David liked Rain better. At least she wasn't a spoiled suburban brat.

Chapter Nine

◆

Maddy woke up at six and lay in bed for fifteen minutes, convincing herself that she was going back to sleep. The morning had dawned clear and cool, the sun burning the dew off of the sagebrush as it climbed higher in the sky. Her porch cricket had long since quieted down—or gone to do whatever crickets do during the day—and the room was as peaceful and silent as a church. The pale sunlight painted patterns on the sheets, and the fresh breeze blew across her cheeks from the open porch doors.

She dreaded having to see David again. It was going to be humiliating. But there wasn't any way around it. It wasn't like she had a whole lot of other options or a choice about whom she'd be spending her days with.

Maddy got up, leaving the sheets in a wad at the end of the bed, and pulled on a pair of Sevens and her favorite American Apparel scoop-neck tee. She braided her hair, letting the end hang over her shoulder before tiptoeing down the stairs to the silent early-morning kitchen.

The room had a tidy, expectant feeling. Debbie's collection of pottery vases on the windowsill stood in the sun like a still life. Maddy dumped coffee into the coffeemaker and leaned her elbows on the counter, listening to the burbling and watching dark brown droplets stream into the glittering glass carafe. It felt good to be up. She realized that she was humming under her breath.

When the coffee was ready, Maddy poured it into a thick blue ceramic mug and wrapped a roll from last night in a napkin. She pushed through the screen door and paused a moment on the porch, sipping her coffee and looking at the mist shrouding the grapevines before making her away across the grass to a path through the fields. The sandy soil felt soft under her feet, and the grape leaves brushed her bare arms, leaving little streaks of wet on her smooth, tanned skin. In front of her, birds took flight at her approach, calling into the cool morning air above the vines before wheeling back around to perch on the trellises.

Maddy reached the edge of the field and approached the shed in the clearing. But instead of going in, she wandered over to the stream and climbed onto a rock, still cool from the night. She brought her knees up to her chest and rested her coffee mug against her leg. Taking a giant bite of her roll, she stared idly at the tangled field in front of her and the mountains beyond, draped in the last strands of the morning fog. The warming sun baked the top of her head.

"Hi," said a voice behind her. "You're up early."

Maddy started, nearly falling off her rock into the stream. She turned around, her mouth still full of bread. David's curly hair looked like he had combed it with a fork, and he was wearing baggy khaki shorts and one of his apparently endless supply of holey T-shirts. He held a foil-wrapped plate in his hand.

"Hello," Maddy said, trying not to spray crumbs. She pointedly looked away and swallowed.

"I made you some cookies."

What? She whipped her head around, trying not to betray her surprise.

"Chocolate-chip apricot. Your mom said you were a chocolate girl."

She couldn't help it. "You talked to my *mom*?"

"Well, I had to find out what you like." He widened his eyes innocently and took the foil off the plate. Big, beautiful cookies studded with dark chunks of chocolate and bits of orange apricot were arranged in a pile.

Maddy sat uncertainly for a second. Of course she

was still mad, but man, those cookies looked good. Without her mind's consent, her hand reached out and took one. She bit into it.

Ohmygod—moist, fantastically chewy, and not too sweet. The melted chocolate chips pulled apart in goopy strands. The apricot bits added perfectly tart little zings. She finished it in about three bites and looked up. David was watching her closely.

"Well?" he asked, a grin playing at the corners of his mouth, waiting for her approval. Maddy forced her face into a frown. *This is the guy who was laughing at you, remember?*

"Um, good," she offered uncertainly. This wasn't how she'd pictured her morning starting.

David smiled widely. "Cool." He pushed the plate into her hands and strode over to the shed. The big doors rumbled as he shoved them open.

Just ignore him, she thought as she carefully climbed down from the rock, brushing the last roll crumbs from her lap and placing the empty coffee mug and the plate of cookies on the ground. She joined him in the doorway. The shed looked about a hundred times better. *He cleaned while I was getting my seaweed wrap,* Maddy thought semi-guiltily. But it still didn't make up for his rudeness last night, even if he *had* made her cookies.

He must have found soap somewhere, because the floors, walls, and windows all gleamed. The place had the feel of a blank canvas. She strolled around the edges of the room, running her fingers over the smooth plaster walls and gazing through the rafters at the soaring peaked roof above. She took a deep breath, inhaling the mixture of wildflowers, soap, and old wood that permeated the air.

"Hey, listen." David walked over slowly and stood in front of her.

She watched him warily. "What?"

"Those cookies?" He paused and stuck his hands in his front pockets.

"Yeah?"

He took a deep breath. "Well, they're sort of a bribe."

"What are you talking about?" She narrowed her eyes.

"I'm trying to bribe you to forgive me for last night." His voice was steady and calm, but his eyes looked anxious as he waited for her reaction. "I don't know what was wrong with me. I acted like a total jerk."

Maddy's face grew warm, but standing in the clear morning light, with David's sincere eyes looking straight into hers, it was hard to summon up the righteous anger that had coursed through her the night before. David dropped his chin, pouted his mouth, and looked at her with pleading, puppy-dog eyes. He looked so ridiculous and adorable that Maddy couldn't help cracking a smile.

"Whatever. Let's just forget it." She turned away, but it was too late.

"I saw that!" he said. "Come here." Before she could react, he had pulled her against his chest in a quick hug.

She jumped and pulled back. "Um—like I said, just forget it. It's no big deal," Maddy mumbled, completely thrown off balance by the sensation of his strong, wiry arms wrapped around her. She brushed uselessly at her hair. Her hands felt like big, awkward paws. She crossed and uncrossed her arms on her chest. *Get a grip!* she instructed herself. *You're acting like a sixth grader.*

"So!" she said, backing up and trying for a breezy tone. "What's the plan for today?" She perched on a barrel and crossed her legs.

David shrugged and sat down on a barrel opposite her. He tilted back, balancing it on its edge. "Honestly? I have no idea. I've only seen a couple tasting rooms before. What are they supposed to look like?"

"You think *I* know? I saw my first grapevine two days ago. It's a room where people drink wine, right? So, like, tables, chairs, pictures on the walls . . ."

David nodded in agreement. "Maybe something to hold the wine bottles, like a rack or some shelves. . . . Hey, wait! I have an awesome idea!" He jumped up. "There are tons of vineyards around here. We should go check some of them out—like a scouting trip. You know, see what the competition is doing with their tasting rooms."

Maddy considered this. It *was* kind of a good idea. She had no idea how to begin, and anyway, it would be better than staying inside all day. She shrugged and rose from her barrel. "Okay. At least we'll get some ideas." She headed toward the door. "The truck was gone this morning. I can get the keys to the Lexus though if—what?"

David's face lit up. "I have a better idea."

✦ ✦ ✦

"You are insane!" Maddy shrieked as she pelted down the hill, David and his bicycle rapidly receding in front of her. The wind whipped her hair back from her face. She gripped her handlebars tightly and lifted her feet from the pedals, letting them spin madly on their own as the wheels hummed faster and faster. The black asphalt of the road seemed to rise up in front of her. "I'm going to diiieeee!" she yelled into the wind.

In front of her, she could see David reach the bottom of the hill and stop, resting one foot on the ground as he turned to watch her. "Ohmygod!" she panted, coasting up next to him. "That was so amazing!" She couldn't keep her face from splitting into a huge grin.

"Bikes are the absolute best way to get around Napa," he said. "My buddies and I once rode from San Francisco all the way up here—that'll be our next trip."

Maddy leaned over the handlebars and tried to catch her breath. "Okay, sure. Just as soon as my heart attack's over."

David snorted laughter and their eyes met. Silence filled the moment, and then Maddy tore her gaze away. She could feel herself blushing a little.

"Look!" She pointed to a sign across the street. "Isn't that the one we were going to look at?"

"Oh, yeah. I've always wanted to see this vineyard. It's supposed to be really fancy."

After pedaling up a long, winding driveway, bordered on both sides by manicured lawns, they left their bikes next to a huge wrought-iron arch and followed the signs to the tasting room. It was in a massive stone building that resembled a medieval castle.

"This is where the knights of California lived in the Middle Ages," David stage-whispered as they entered. Maddy stifled a giggle and pushed open the tasting room door. A few sunburned tourists in shorts looked around as they entered but after a cursory glance quickly buried their noses in their glasses of wine.

"What do you think?" Maddy asked David in a low voice. He swept the room with his gaze, taking in the high, dark wood bar that stood at one end, the brass railing and fixtures, the stained-glass windows, and the thick, dark red rugs that covered the stone floor. He grimaced.

"I feel like I should be asking forgiveness for something," he muttered back.

She nodded. "It does feel like a church—not like California at all."

"Yeah, it actually makes me want to fall asleep, not buy wine." He pointed to a huge leather couch. "That's my nap spot right there."

"All right, let's go," Maddy said, pushing open the door again. "I think they'd kick us out if you curled up on their couch."

Back in the bright sunshine, they mounted their bikes again. "Okay, the next one's about two miles up the road," David said, standing up on the pedals. He glanced at Maddy, who was fiddling with her gear lever. "You think you can make it, little girl?"

Maddy looked up sharply, her eyes flashing with momentary anger. Then she saw his laughing face and grinned. "No, can you cawwy me, big, strong man?" she asked in a little-girl whine. Without waiting for a response, she leaned low over the handlebars and pushed off, pedaling as fast as she could. She didn't look back for the first mile, expecting at any moment to hear the hum of David's bike approaching behind her. But she didn't, and when she stopped for a breather after a mile and a half, she saw that he was still a couple hundred yards back, pedaling hard. He rode up next to her, panting.

"You know," he said, wiping his damp face with the

bottom of his T-shirt and briefly revealing a flat, chiseled stomach, "I wish you wouldn't hold me back like this. It's really going to be a problem."

Maddy tried to ignore his abs and concentrated on redoing her ponytail. "Sorry," she replied airily. "I'll try to speed up next time."

They rode slowly, side by side for the last half mile. The wind was still and the road was deserted. A lone black-and-white cow stared at them balefully from behind a rail fence.

A trickle of sweat coursed down the side of Maddy's face. "Whew!" she breathed when they finally reached the hand-drawn sign of their next vineyard. She eyed the white squeeze bottle strapped to the crossbar of David's bike. "Can I have some of that?"

"Sure." He pulled the bottle from its holder and handed it to her. She tilted her head back and squirted a long stream of water into her open mouth. Out of the corner of her eye, she could see David watching her. She took quick aim and squeezed the bottle hard, catching him right in the face.

"Hey!" he sputtered, laughing a little and wiping his face with his forearm. "What was that for?"

Maddy smiled with satisfaction. "For calling me a snob. Now we're even." She leaned over and stuck the water bottle back on his bike. "Shall we?"

The tasting room was just inside the vineyard

entrance. "This reminds me of a Marriott," Maddy murmured as they stared inside. The room was tiled in beige and white, with a light wood bar and some long, modern tables. The walls were partially glass, which flooded the space with light, but it hardly felt cozy.

"Actually," David said, "the lobby of my grandma's retirement home kind of looks like this." His voice echoed against the high ceiling. The redheaded woman behind the bar shot them a dirty look.

"Look," Maddy whispered, "we've made a friend already." The redhead was polishing wineglasses while glaring at them.

She cleared her throat. "If you want to taste wine, you'll have to show proper ID," she called in a nasal voice.

"Shoot!" David slapped his forehead with the heel of his hand. "Of all the days to forget my wallet! I guess we'll have to skip this one."

The woman scowled and Maddy grabbed David's elbow. "Thanks anyway!" she called, and hustled out the door. She dropped her hand once they were outside and punched him on the bicep. "Nice going, Mr. Suave."

David shrugged and grinned down at her. "She's just mad because her tasting room looks like an old folks' home."

Maddy realized that they were walking companionably down the vineyard path together, side by side, their arms swinging easily and their hands almost touching. What had happened this afternoon? She'd been prepared to be furious but then he'd caught her off guard with those cookies. And all of the biking and scouting had turned out to be pretty fun. *You're still in Napa,* Maddy reminded herself. *"Fun" is relative.* Her BlackBerry beeped in her pocket, interrupting her thoughts. She glanced at the screen: Kirsten.

"Hey," she answered breezily.

"Ohmygod, are you totally miserable?" her friend squealed in her ear.

"We miss you soooo much!" a voice called from the background.

"Tell Morgan I miss her too," Maddy said. "Yeah, it sucks up here." Some part of her felt sort of guilty saying that, like she was lying or something. She didn't look at David. "I'm, um, getting used to it though."

"Do you—" There was a crash on the other end of the phone and some scuffling. Morgan came on the line, panting a little.

"I told Kirsten *I* wanted to talk," she said. "So, have you met any hotties to keep you busy?"

"Um, not really." She glanced at David, who had already reached the bikes and was fiddling with his lock.

Morgan sighed. "Too bad."

"Yeah, well, I'll survive, I think."

David looked up at Maddy and opened his mouth to

say something. She flapped her hand at him and turned her back quickly. "Look, *chica*, I have to go—call you later, okay?" She pressed END before Morgan could respond. She walked over to the bikes.

"So, it's one already," David said, glancing at his Swiss Army watch. "What's our next adventure?"

Maddy couldn't believe how fast the morning had gone, and that she'd actually had a good time. She swung her leg over her bike. "I don't know about you, but my next adventure is to find some lunch—I'm starving."

David mounted his bike also and followed her slowly down the road back toward home. "Well," he said from behind her, "we could go eat at your place, if that's okay with you."

Surprised, Maddy turned partly around to look back at him, causing her bike to wobble dangerously. "Um, sure," she said cautiously. "That'd be okay."

Chapter Ten

❖

Back at the house, Maddy hurriedly peered into the fridge while David was upstairs washing his hands. Tuna salad was too messy. Leftover homemade pizza? Not very appealing—she'd smell like garlic. Then she stopped. Why did it matter if she smelled like garlic or stinky feet or Thierry Mugler Angel, for that matter? She had just grabbed the jar of Skippy when she heard David's footsteps thumping down the stairs.

"PB&J?" he asked, eyeing the jar in her hand. The curls at his hairline were damp from washing his face. His skin glowed from the sun and the exertion of the morning. Maddy wondered if he'd somehow brushed his teeth too, because he smelled fresh and minty. She shrugged, frowning at the peanut butter jar.

"I can't think of anything else." She took the bread from the stainless-steel bread box on the counter.

"Hmm." David stared into the fridge. He quickly pulled out a plastic tub of olives, a wedge of hard white cheese with a red rind, and a bowl of radishes. He set everything on the counter and gently took the bread from her hand. Maddy stood in the middle of the floor, staring like an idiot. She shook herself and sat down at the table, watching David inspect the bread.

"Nice sourdough baguette—someone in your house has good taste," he said, ripping off two big hunks and wrapping them in a paper towel.

"I guess this means you're making lunch," Maddy said from her spectator's seat. David glanced over.

"If you don't mind . . ."

She held her hands up. "Be my guest."

He sliced the cheese and radishes and put them in a plastic Tupperware container. Then he searched through the drawers until he found a short, thin knife and chopped the olives into bits, his hands moving quickly and confidently. He mixed the chopped olives with a little olive oil, a squeeze of a lemon from the bowl on the windowsill, and a smashed clove of garlic and spooned the whole mess into another container.

"A little olive tapenade for our bread and cheese," he said, turning to Maddy, who realized she had been watching with her mouth hanging open a little. She shut it abruptly and got up.

"Wow," she managed. "Definitely better than PB&J." David grinned at her and started stuffing things into a grocery bag. They grabbed bottles of cold SmartWater from the fridge, and by tacit consent headed out through the vines to the banks of the little stream.

For a while after they plopped down on the soft grass and spread out the food, they just chewed quietly, staring straight ahead. Some of the ease of the morning had disappeared, and the silence stretched out until it became a little awkward. Maddy surreptitiously glanced over at David. He was picking through the container of radishes. He flicked one with a brown spot away over his shoulder. Maddy flipped her hair behind her shoulders and took a bite of the thick, chewy bread and tangy cheese. "So, did you grow up around here?" It came out a little snotty-sounding and she winced. But either he didn't notice or he was pretending not to.

"Yeah—but now I only live here in the summers. During the year, I go to Westside Public in San Francisco."

"Really? I didn't know you were from the city."

He shrugged. "Yeah. I live with my aunt and uncle during the school year. My dad didn't think any of the schools in Napa were up to his standards." He took an enormous bite of bread and cheese and chewed with his cheeks puffed out.

Maddy dipped into the olive tapenade. "This is really good, by the way," she told him. "So, do you hate the city or what?"

He looked startled. "No, I love the city. What made you think I hate it?"

"Well, I mean, you really seem to love it up here— messing around with the shed, riding bikes."

"You didn't like the bikes?"

"No! I did! It was fun, but it's so different back home."

He shrugged and pressed the top back on the empty container of tapenade. Stretching his long legs out in front of him, he answered, "It *is* different. But my friends and I bike all the time in the city. There are some amazing trails. I have friends up here, too, but it's obviously way more fun to go out in the city. Napa doesn't exactly have a rockin' nightlife, in case you wondered."

Maddy giggled. "Hanging out with the cricket on my porch doesn't count as an awesome night out?"

"Are you kidding? Up here, that would get you on Page Six. But I like all the space up here." He gestured to the flower-strewn field in front of them and the acres of vines at their backs.

Maddy let out a little snort. "There's definitely enough of that around here."

"Yeah. It'd be nice to have a little more space in our house though." He took a long drink of water and leaned back on his hands.

"Where do you guys live?" she asked, feeling a little silly for not knowing.

"Stand up for a second." They both climbed to their feet. Maddy brushed the dried grass off her pants. "Now look over there." David put his hand on her shoulder and turned her to the left. She started a little and jerked before she could stop herself. David dropped his hand and looked at her curiously. She laughed a little and pretended to brush more grass off her jeans. *Why are you acting like a nervous kid, Madeline?*

She steadied herself. "What am I looking for?"

He pointed. "Do you see that little bit of white through the trees?" Maddy didn't respond. She was distracted by the strong line of David's jaw, sprinkled with a shadow of dark stubble.

He was staring at her too. She dragged her attention back to the tree line. "Oh, yeah, I do." She strained her eyes to see through a stand of pines farther down the stream. "Kind of."

"That's our place. It's in Jenkins's field. He's a farmer—"

"Yeah, I kind of know him, or at least, I know who he is," Maddy interrupted. "I've met his, um, pig." She didn't elaborate. David looked perplexed. "It's a long story."

"Well, he's a really nice guy. My dad rented a cottage

on his property this winter. He does some maintenance on his tractors and things in return for a cut on the rent. It's a pretty small place, but we don't have a lot of stuff— you know, two guys alone and everything."

The obvious question hung in the air, but Maddy didn't ask it. They sat down again and David poked at the grass with a twig. "My mom lives in L.A. They got divorced when I was little."

She nodded. "That's too bad."

"It's okay. It was a really long time ago."

They were quiet for a minute. Maddy changed the subject. "So, where'd you learn to cook?"

"At Mondavi. My dad was the vineyard manager there for years. I was always hanging around the kitchen when I was a little kid, asking for snacks, being annoying. Finally, the line cooks started giving me stuff to do so I'd quit bothering them. I washed vegetables, but they eventually let me do some chopping. When I was fifteen they let me come on as an intern."

Maddy shook her head and shifted so that she was sitting cross-legged. She watched an ant carry a dead beetle through the grass in front of her. "That's so cool. I've never known a guy my age who *could* cook, much less liked to."

David heaved a mock-tired sigh. "I know. My friends call me Emeril, but they're more than happy to eat whatever I make."

"I'm a hopeless cook," Maddy confessed. "I max out at spaghetti and scrambled eggs."

"I love scrambled eggs," David said, his hand on his chest. "How did you know that's my favorite food in the world?"

"Scrambled eggs are your favorite food?"

"Well, no," David said, grinning a little devilishly. "Actually, my favorite food is steamed lobster. I was just trying to make you feel better."

Maddy laughed. "Thanks a lot, jerk!" She shoved him onto the grass. He fell on his side with a thud and curled up in a ball.

"Help!" he moaned to the air in front of him. "Assault! This girl is beating me up! The only thing that'll save me is . . . is . . . a chocolate-chip cookie!" He continued moaning pitifully.

Maddy couldn't help laughing at him. "Okay!" she said, half crawling over to the plate of cookies still sitting by the rock where she'd left them this morning. She broke one in half.

"Help! Time is running out!" David, with his eyes still closed, opened his mouth like a fish. Maddy poked in the cookie, stuffing the other half into her own mouth.

He sat up. "Ahh, much better," he managed through the cookie. Maddy's phone beeped from the grass between them. "Wow, you're popular!" He reached across Maddy's lap and swiped the phone. "Who could this be? Call from Brian—who's Brian, your boyfriend?" he teased.

"David, give me that!" In a panic, Maddy grabbed at the phone, but he held it just out of her reach, grinning. "Hallooo, Pierre's Auto Repair, who ees dis?" he cried in a high falsetto. He winked at Maddy.

"Stop! Give it to me!" she hissed furiously. David must have seen something change in her face. His grin faded and he handed the phone back.

"Sorry," he mouthed. Maddy glared at him angrily and jogged a few feet away, turning her back.

"Hi," she said.

"Who the hell was that?" Brian did not sound happy.

"No one—just this guy I'm working with." Maddy tried to make her voice unruffled. She peeked over her shoulder. David was throwing small stones into the stream, staring straight ahead of him.

"There's a *guy* up there? Thanks for telling me."

"I didn't have a chance! Anyway, you have nothing to worry about. He's the son of my dad's business partner, so just calm down, okay?"

"I'm not mad that there's a guy up there—I'm mad because you didn't say anything about it." Brian's voice rose.

"Okay, okay!" Maddy glanced at David nervously. "I can't talk right now."

"Whatever," Brian said sullenly. "Have fun with that asshole."

"Look, stop. I'll call you later, okay?"

"Yeah, if you can fit me into your busy schedule." He hung up. Maddy stood still for a second, breathing a little hard. Then she turned back toward David, who was watching her as he tried to juggle three little stones.

"Hey, look, I've almost got this—"

"Why did you do that?" Maddy demanded. The force of her words surprised her.

He caught the stones and stared at her, his mouth open a little.

"That was really inconsiderate, David!" she cried.

He blinked. "Sorry." He held his hands up like he was surrendering. "It was just a joke. Why are you so mad?"

"That was my boyfriend, idiot!"

"Ohh," he said, realization dawning on his face. He fell back a few steps. "Wow. Sorry."

"You already said that." Maddy turned around, trying to control herself. Why was she freaking out? It *was* just a stupid joke. She usually didn't get so upset about things like this. She shook her head. "Look, I'm just tired. It's been a long morning."

David nodded in agreement. "Yeah." He looked at her as if he was seeing something different. "Tell your boyfriend I'm sorry the next time you talk to him."

"Sure," Maddy agreed. They stared at each other for a second. As David turned around and headed toward the little house in the next field, Maddy's stomach sank. Their houses were only a field apart, but they lived in totally different worlds.

Chapter Eleven

✦

Maddy wandered along the sidewalk. After a couple of awkwardly quiet cleaning days with David, she had decided she needed a little alone time when she woke up this morning. A bike ride into town and a little retail therapy were just what she needed to clear her head.

Maddy stopped and gazed into a boutique window. A gauzy, deconstructed silk dress floated from a hanger. She squinted at the price tag: $1,500. For something that looked like a cat had tangled with it? She snorted and walked on.

The next shop was all hand-milled local soaps, body scrubs, and perfumes. *Mmm.* Maddy inhaled the scent of bergamot floating from the open door. But as she moved toward the entrance, she caught a flutter of cloth out of the corner of her eye. She turned around. A stall was set up across the street, with large, heavy rugs hanging from horizontal poles. The strong breeze sent a few swaying gently back and forth. Maddy started to turn back to the soap store, but something about the rugs made her turn around again and cross the street.

"Hi," she said to the little woman sitting in the stall. The woman's hair hung in a long gray braid over one shoulder, and her face was as wrinkled as a raisin. But her eyes were shiny black and sparkled with mischief. She smiled at Maddy and nodded.

"I weave all of these myself," she said in a gravelly voice, gesturing to the huge pieces of fabric hanging around her like a Bedouin tent.

"They're beautiful," Maddy said automatically, fingering one. Then she looked more closely. They really *were* beautiful: thick and heavy, with rich colors that glowed like jewels. They were unusual, too. Some were woven flat and neatly bound, but others were fantasy creations with metallic fabrics and odd shapes. Maddy bent to examine one huge rustic concoction of cream and brown wool. Strips of fabric hung off it at various points, accentuating its rough, uneven border.

"That was one of the first rugs I wove," the woman said, watching Maddy. "No one is ever interested in it— it's quite unusual."

"Yeah," Maddy said slowly. "It is. I like it, though."

The woman nodded. "Good eye," she said appreciatively.

An idea was beginning to form in Maddy's head. She pictured the rug flung over the scrubbed floorboards of the tasting room, patches of sunlight dancing over the weave. It was perfect for the space. "How much is it?" She hardly dared to ask. The woman considered and Maddy held her breath.

"Five hundred," the woman finally declared. Maddy exhaled. That was well within her decorating budget.

"I'll take it," she said. "Can you deliver?"

"My son delivers in his truck, but he won't be back until next month." They arranged the delivery date and payment and shook hands. Maddy walked back across the street, her heart still beating fast from the excitement of the purchase. *Just wait until David sees it,* she thought. She was so immersed in mentally arranging the tasting room that she walked right past the soap store without even realizing it.

As she was starting on the bike ride home, her phone rang in her pocket. Maddy managed to answer without falling over.

"So, guess where Taylor and Sunny are going for vacation this summer?" Morgan asked without preamble.

"Oh my God, don't tell me—Baghdad." Maddy grinned into her phone, trying to steer with one hand.

"You're hilarious. They're going to Dubai," Morgan replied.

"Dubai?" Maddy squealed.

"Supposedly, it's amazing—better beaches than Maui."

Maddy's bike gave a big wobble and an approaching delivery van honked at her and swerved. "Hold on," she told Morgan, and swung off onto the golden grass at the side of the road. Sticking the phone in her pocket momentarily, she hauled the bike over an irrigation ditch and propped it against a wooden fence post. She sank down onto the dry, fragrant grass and dug the phone out again. She could hear Morgan take a deep breath to go on with the details of Sunny and Taylor in Dubai, but suddenly, Maddy felt like she just *had* to say something.

"Hey," she cut Morgan off. "Remember when you asked me if I'd met any hotties up here and I said no?"

Morgan screeched. Maddy held the phone slightly away from her ear. "There *is* a hot guy up there! I knew there had to be at least one in all of Napa Valley. Who is it?"

Maddy stared across the empty strip of asphalt before her. On the other side of the road was another wooden fence just like the one she was leaning against. "A guy from up here. His name's David; he's the son of my dad's partner on the vineyard. We've been working together on this tasting room."

"Have you been a good girl so far? *I* wouldn't be."

"Do you ever think of anything else?" Maddy asked, rolling her eyes.

"What else is there?"

"Very funny. And the answer is yes, for your information. Of course I've been a good girl. But here's the weird thing." Maddy filled Morgan in on the details of the phone encounter. "So I freaked out for nothing and now Brian's mad at me," she finished. "This place is messing with my mind."

"Well, it *was* annoying that he grabbed your phone like that," Morgan comforted her. "Honestly, though? It sounds like he was flirting with you."

"*What?*" Maddy squeaked. "You're insane!" Her mind flitted back to David's "spoiled suburban brat" remark the night of the dinner party. She shook her head. "Mor, believe me, this guy has no desire to flirt with me."

"If you say so," Morgan replied. "But it sure sounds like flirting to me, and I should know." She laughed. Maddy felt irritated. For practically the first time ever, her friend didn't seem to get it.

"Look, he wasn't, okay?" she said, more sharply than she intended.

"Okay, Mads, chill out," Morgan said.

Maddy took a deep breath and changed the subject. "Hey, guess what I found in town today?"

"What?"

"The perfect rug for the tasting room!" Maddy said excitedly. She waited for Morgan's reaction.

"Um, great," Morgan said.

"Yeah, isn't that cool?" Maddy prompted. "It's pretty unusual. I haven't actually seen one like it before and the woman selling them said it was one of the first she'd ever made."

"Awesome," Morgan replied. "I've never know you to get this worked up over a rug before, Mad. Are you turning into a little Martha Stewart?"

Maddy forced a laugh. "Of course not. It's just that, well, it's a really cool rug—and I'm kind of having fun thinking about fixing up this room. Listen, I'm getting all itchy sitting here in the grass. I'll call you later, okay?"

"Okay, bye, Martha." Morgan chortled, and clicked off. Maddy stuck her phone back in her pocket violently and grabbed her bike. She rode off, pumping hard on the pedals, even though the road was flat.

✦ ✦ ✦

The rosy shadows of dusk were gathering among the grapevines when Maddy rode up the long gravel driveway. The ride home had taken longer than she expected. She was halfway to the house when she saw

David's gray pickup approaching. She stopped, still straddling the bike, and waved. As he pulled up next to her and leaned out of the open window, Morgan's words flitted through her mind: *"He was flirting with you."* Maddy looked at David carefully. He didn't seem different, just cheerful and glad to see her.

"Hey, listen," he said. "I'm glad I ran into you. I wanted to tell you again what an idiot I was to grab your phone like that. Can you just chalk it up to me being a boneheaded guy?"

Maddy smiled back at him, tossing back her wind-tousled hair. "You're forgiven, bonehead," she said. "By the way, you're going to love me even more after what I did this afternoon."

"What, ran off to the spa again?" he teased.

"No, jerk!" She playfully punched his elbow resting on the truck window. "I found the ultimate piece for the tasting room. It's going to totally make the look."

"No way," he replied enthusiastically, getting out of the car. "I didn't know you were shopping for us this afternoon."

"Um . . . yeah, I was," Maddy said. He didn't have to know her real reason for going into town.

"So? What is it? I can't stand the suspense." He flicked a mosquito away from Maddy's shoulder.

"It's–" She stopped abruptly. "Actually, I think I'm

not going to tell you. It'll be a surprise when it's delivered."

"You're heartless!" he said, clutching his chest.

Maddy prepared to pedal off. "See you at the Robertsons' tomorrow night," she said. Everyone had been invited to a pre-harvest dinner party at the Robertsons' vineyard down the road, celebrating the successful maturation of the grapes.

"I don't think I'm going to go," David told her. "I kind of feel like just crashing on the couch for a night."

"Oh," Maddy said, surprised by the disappointment that washed over her at his words. *Why do you care, Maddy?* the voice in her head asked. *Well, I don't,* she told herself. *He can do whatever he wants.* "See you later, then," she said, her voice purposefully airy.

"Do you want a ride back? The bugs are getting pretty nasty out here." He didn't wait for her response as he reached for her bike.

"Oh, sure. Thanks." She watched his strong arms lift the bike onto the truck bed as she climbed into the passenger seat.

The ride was short, and neither of them spoke much. But the quiet between them wasn't awkward. In fact, as Maddy leaned against the worn seat, she realized she couldn't remember the last time she'd felt this at ease.

After they pulled up to the house, Maddy stood on the porch steps as David retrieved her bike from the back of the truck. He revved the engine, waving as he drove off down the driveway. Not that Maddy wanted him to stay longer. She was much too good a girl for that.

Chapter Twelve

✦

Mouth agape, Maddy stared up at the Robertsons' concrete and glass house in front of her. "What *is* this place? A huge sculpture?" she whispered to her mother, who was examining the twenty-foot steel-beamed ceiling.

"A lot of the vineyards up here are doing an ultra-modern thing," her mother whispered back. "I feel like I'm inside a Picasso." They wandered up the remainder of the stone path to the house, with Dad following behind. All around them, little knots of well-dressed wine lovers stood chatting, long-stemmed glasses in hand, or strolled through the fields, inspecting the fruit and vine leaves. A buzz of conversation rose above the murmur of the evening wind in the treetops and mixed with the heavy scent of grapes that hung in the air.

For a nice change, Maddy was feeling annoyed with Brian. He hadn't called since their spat on the phone, and Maddy was determined not to be the first to call. She hadn't done anything wrong! She jumped out of the way as she walked practically on top of a girl examining some flowers at the side of the path. The girl straightened up and turned toward Maddy and her parents, the automatic smile fading from her face.

Maddy narrowed her eyes. "Hi, Rain," she said deliberately. She was pleased to see the girl blush a little. She should, after the porch incident. But Maddy's fleeting sense of triumph faded fast.

"Hi," Rain said smoothly, tossing her hair over one shoulder. She met Maddy's gaze coolly and confidently, with no hint of embarrassment.

Maddy gritted her teeth. Her mom tapped her shoulder. "Daddy and I are going to say hi to the Robertsons," she said. "We'll see you inside." They strolled away, hand in hand.

Thanks a lot, Mom, Maddy thought as silence descended. She was stranded. Walking away now would make her look like a complete doofus. "How's it going?" she asked in her frostiest voice, pretending to inspect the red flowers on a tree next to her. Really, though, she was eyeing Rain's outfit. Once again, she'd gone with the outdoorsy look: sage green cotton sun-dress, thin leather flip-flops, and a simple silver bangle on one wrist. Her hair was done in two loose, tousled braids. Maddy fidgeted with the tie of her own black jersey wrap dress. It had seemed so elegant when she put it on an hour ago, but now it felt stuffy next to Rain's earth-girl freshness.

"Great!" Rain said aggressively. More silence, which was broken by the sound of a woman calling from the house.

"Dinner is served! Fresh tomatoes are waiting!" Laughing and talking, guests began streaming up the path in twos and threes, clutching their glasses, the women picking their way carefully in high heels. Rain turned with a huff and flounced toward the house. Maddy tried to look nonchalant as she followed, attempting to squash the miserable anger welling up inside her.

Dinner was buffet-style, so Maddy was able to avoid Rain completely, for which she was profoundly grateful. Proximity to that witch would've spoiled her appetite, and she planned to enjoy her rare sirloin.

After filling her plate, Maddy perched next to her parents on an overstuffed bench on the expansive teak patio. She thought she might broach the subject of her birthday again. She'd been so good recently—working on the tasting room, helping around the house, not complaining. Dad had already said the shed looked even better than he had thought it would. They had to let her go to the city. Her annoyance with Brian faded as she smiled to herself, thinking of seeing him in San Francisco. It would make up for all of this work if she could just have a weekend alone with him, she thought, spearing a piece of nicely browned potato. She took a deep breath. "Um, guys."

Her mom looked up from her steak. She smiled fondly at her daughter. "Yes, sweetheart?"

"Well, I was thinking about my birthday. . . ." Mom looked at Dad and set down her fork. Maddy rushed ahead. "And you know how I had mentioned maybe I could go down to the city for a couple of days? Or just overnight?" she added hastily, seeing her mother open her mouth as if to object. "I mean, you know, since the tasting room is looking so good—right, Dad? A couple of days off wouldn't hurt."

Maddy's mother sighed and set her plate on the glass table in front of her. She looked at her husband. He chewed thoughtfully. "Maddy, you know it's not about the work up here," he said. "You've done a wonderful job so far—your mother and I have been very impressed. But of course, we're concerned about what happened before. You know that's why we're reluctant to let you go to the city."

Maddy's stomach plunged. "Dad, please! I know it

was stupid to throw that party—I totally admit it! But how long are you going to punish me for it? Haven't I shown you I can be responsible?" Her voice rose. A couple sitting a few feet away looked around curiously, but Maddy was too upset to care.

Her dad shook his head. "Maddy, it's not just the party. We have to wonder what other rules you'd disregard if we were to let you go back there alone. It's time for you to show us that you understand what it means to be a part of this family. We know you miss Brian and Morgan and Kirsten, but your mom and I think it would best if you had just a small, family celebration for your birthday this year. We can do something low-key—maybe go into town for dinner and see a movie, all three of us." He offered this like it was some sort of treat.

Maddy could feel her face getting red. "Dinner and a movie with my parents? Thanks a lot, guys! That sounds like a great seventeenth birthday! While you're at it, why don't the two of you go ahead and buy a vineyard in Napa and then drag me up here all summer without considering what *I* was planning for *my* summer? Oh, I'm sorry, *you already did that!*" She saw a hurt look cross her mother's face.

Maddy leaped up from the bench, almost knocking the glass table over in the process. Ignoring the wide-eyed stares of the people around her, she fled into the house, angry tears starting in her eyes. She looked wildly around for a bathroom and spotted it through a half-open door. She darted in, turning the lock behind her, and stared furiously into the mirror. Her face, red and blotchy, stared back at her. *They're holding me prisoner here,* she thought. Who knew what this would do to her relationship with Brian? He wasn't going to be happy about it, that was for sure. He was probably going to forget about her, stuck up here in this pit! Maddy sat down on the closed toilet seat and reached for a tissue. She was going to lose her boyfriend over her parents' stupid vineyard, and it was all their fault.

She couldn't spend all evening in the bathroom, so after a few minutes, Maddy splashed some cold water on her face and dried it with a soft blue hand towel. Gazing at her reflection again, she took deep breaths to get her heart rate under control. She rubbed on a little lip gloss and combed her hair. There. Now at least she didn't *look* hysterical.

Maddy opened the bathroom door and ran smack into David, who was standing right outside. "What are you doing here?" She gasped.

He scratched his curly head. He was wearing a fitted navy blue polo shirt that skimmed his chest and khakis with Reef flip-flops. It was the first time Maddy had seen him in anything but an old T-shirt and jeans. *He looks good,* she thought to herself. "I'm staking out the bathroom to see if I can pick up chicks," he told her. "See? It worked."

Maddy laughed, totally forgetting about her foul mood. "I thought you weren't coming tonight," she said. David led the way to a striped sofa in a corner of the huge, packed living room.

"I decided I was in the mood for free food after all. Anyway, you can only watch ESPN Classic for so long before your brain starts melting." He stretched his legs out in front of him and laced his fingers behind his head. "Nice place, huh?" he said, taking in the white armchairs, white rugs, and geometric black-and-white paintings on the walls.

Maddy shrugged. "If you like this sort of thing. I'm more into–"

"Hey, David."

They both craned around. Rain stood just behind the sofa, a frosty glass of mint lemonade in hand and a broad smile pasted on her face. "Oh, hi, Rain," David replied. Maddy glanced quickly at his face. He looked relaxed and friendly as always but not particularly excited. Rain came around to the front of the couch and threw herself down into one of the white armchairs across from them.

"What's been going on with you?" She directed her question only at David, Maddy noticed bitterly.

"Not much," he said briefly, and turned back to

Maddy. "Did I tell you my brilliant idea for the tasting room? I think I'm going to patent it."

Maddy smiled. "No, what, Einstein?"

"I think we should do little tables instead of one long one."

"They have that over at Smithfield," Rain broke in. "Have you been over there?" She looked at Maddy. "I don't know if you'd be interested. It's pretty . . ." She paused. *"Rustic."* She giggled a little and glanced at David. He shrugged.

"We've been rustic all week, haven't we?" he replied, looking at Maddy instead of Rain. "The bike trip wasn't exactly a luxury ride."

"Not exactly." Maddy was only partly listening to David, though. She was watching Rain's face, which wrinkled with confusion. This clearly wasn't going as she'd expected. And to be honest, it wasn't going as Maddy had expected either. As if to confirm her thoughts, David turned back toward Maddy.

"Next bike trip, I'll show you this amazing little cave my friends and I found one summer."

"Cool . . . ," Maddy said slowly, trying to calm her thoughts. Rain was staring at them, openmouthed. *She* had *loved their bike ride,* Maddy thought. Other than the Brian weirdness, hanging out with David had actually been the highlight of her prison sentence. But he'd been all into Rain at the last party—and now he knew that Maddy had a boyfriend. Everything seemed different somehow. He was practically ignoring Rain. What the hell was going on? Whatever it was, Maddy decided she liked this new situation much better.

Chapter Thirteen

❖

Maddy tucked the edges of the old quilt around the wicker picnic basket so it wouldn't jiggle in the car, and flopped into the backseat. She tugged at her bikini underneath a white C&C California tank top and a pair of ancient Blue Cult jeans.

Her dad was sitting in the driver's seat with the door open, rustling around with a giant map and talking to himself under his breath as he marked a route with a pencil. "Turn onto 17, then down three miles, left at the gas station. . . ."

The whole family was going to a beach nearby. "A nice little outing," Maddy's mom had said. Fred and David were meeting them there. Maddy had had to force herself not to make a remark about what a Napa beach might be like compared to a San Francisco beach, but she'd managed to keep her mouth safely shut. Things between her and her parents had been a little stiff ever since their fight the week before. She hadn't really said much to them since then—just "Please pass the milk," "I'm going to bed," things like that.

She had to admit that it was a gorgeous day. The sky looked freshly washed, and fluffy, woolly clouds floated above in a dignified procession. A mass of flowers had bloomed by the side of the driveway and around the house—purple, red, and blue with splashes of orange. The air smelled like earth and fresh pine.

After about twenty minutes of driving past little grocery stores, vineyards, and farm stands selling melons and blueberries, turning onto progressively smaller and smaller country roads, Bob said, "Debbie, look at the map, will you? I think Fred said it was right past Mason's, but I don't see the—ah!" He jammed on the brakes, jolting Maddy against her seat belt. "Here it is!" Maddy just barely detected a tiny dirt path winding back into the pine forest, just off the road. It was almost hidden by the drooping branches of the massive fir trees lining both sides of the pavement.

She leaned forward as they wound down the tiny, dark road. The forest looked like something out of a creepy fairy tale, with huge trees and tangled grass all around. Barely any sunshine filtered through those enormous branches, leaving the spaces underneath dark and shadowy. Maddy's dad peered through the windshield as he slowly drove down the bumpy dirt road. "Bob, are you sure this is the right one?" Her mother asked, anxiously looking out the window.

"Well, it was right past the shop, like Fred said. Anyway, I think there's a clearing ahead."

Maddy could just see a patch of light at the end of the road. The patch grew larger as they drove until it suddenly widened into a broad, sun-flooded meadow. Switchgrass, heavy with seeds, nodded on each side of the window as the wind blew through the stems. At the base of the meadow, Bob parked next to the gray pickup. Maddy was surprised at how happy she was to see David's long, lean figure climbing down from the cab.

Fred and her parents disappeared down a short path just in front of them. "Hey," Maddy said, greeting David.

He blasted her with the full wattage of his white smile. "Hey, cutie." *What?* David was still talking but Maddy barely heard what he was saying. She felt a dopey grin spread over her face. *Stop it,* she instructed herself. *You do not care that David thinks you're cute. What's with the giddy schoolgirl reaction?* Why did he have this effect on her?

David, oblivious to Maddy's internal drama, reached into the cab of the pickup and pulled out a big hamper.

"You are going to love this lake," he told her. "It's my favorite place in Napa."

"I can't wait to swim," Maddy said, getting a grip on herself. "I haven't been in the water since leaving the city."

The little dirt path wove through the pine trees, twisting right and then left again. Maddy ducked to avoid the low-hanging branches and stepped carefully around a boggy spot in the middle. In another dozen yards, the trees gave way to some shrubs, which opened onto a little beach. The change was so sudden that Maddy stopped short, causing David to bump into her. A small, calm lake spread before them, glistening in the early afternoon sun, completely surrounded by the forest. The sandy beach edged the water and an old, weathered dock extended out from the shore. The air smelled of rich mud and silt. Little crabs ran over the sand and hid in their holes. In the middle of the lake, Maddy saw a silvery splash as a fish jumped toward the sky. Except for the fish, the place was completely deserted.

Her parents were already setting up low lawn chairs and a few pillows. Fred dragged over a big log to serve as a bench. David started unpacking the food. "Look!" Maddy pointed. A peregrine falcon was soaring overhead.

"Those are endangered," David said, taking the tops off of some Tupperware containers.

"I know," Maddy said, spreading out the big green blanket. David did a double take. "Don't look so surprised," she teased.

"I'm not," he said unconvincingly.

"Sure you're not. For your information, I learned all about birds at the Raptor Center back in the city." Maddy eyed him. "See, you're surprised I even know what the Raptor Center is," she said, poking his arm.

"I'm n— Well, okay, I'm a little surprised," he admitted, dumping salad into a big plastic bowl. Several feet away, her parents and Fred were laughing quietly as Fred pointed out something in the sand.

"My friend Kirsten and I took a bird there once." She focused for a moment on balancing five glasses on a flat rock next to her. She looked up and found David watching her expectantly.

"Why?" he prompted. Maddy felt sort of dumb telling this story, but it was too late to change the subject.

"Well, we were driving on 17 last year and this kestrel flew into the windshield of the car right in front of us. We saw it get thrown over to the side of the road. So we stopped on the on-ramp, picked it up, and wrapped it in a towel. It wasn't dead, but it just lay there looking at us with its beak open. Kirsten said we should take it to the Raptor Center—she took a vulture there once." Maddy stopped for a second. David was watching her with his mouth slightly open. "What?"

He shut his mouth abruptly. "Nothing. What happened then?"

"So we took him over there and the technician looked at him and said that he hadn't broken anything but he was in shock from getting hit. They put him in a cage, and at first he kept walking into the bars and falling over. Kirsten and I went back every day to see him until he was ready to be released back into the wild," Maddy finished. She looked at David, feeling a little self-conscious. "If you must know, we named him Harold," she added. David was quiet. He seemed to be thinking about something.

Then he shook his head. "That's cool. I didn't think . . . ," he said, not finishing his sentence.

"Didn't think what?" Maddy asked.

He looked at her a minute longer. "Nothing. Hey, do you want to cut this up?" He handed her a loaf of French bread and a knife.

"Sure." She started slicing onto a large cloth napkin. Their parents wandered over.

"Wow," Dad said, looking at the lunch spread. There was a giant salad of greens with crumbly cheese, apples, and curly arugula. A plate of cold, sliced chicken breast drizzled with tarragon and olive oil sat next to a bowl of raspberries that were a deep, almost luminous red-pink. A big bottle of Perrier, its sides frosty and dripping, stood ready to be opened. Maddy's mouth was watering.

She couldn't help reaching for a berry. She popped the soft little fruit into her mouth.

"Mmmm," she murmured. It was sweet and warm. "How long did it take you to make all of this?" she asked David.

He shrugged. "Not long—it's like the lunch I made you. If you have really good ingredients, the food is better when you mostly leave it alone."

Everyone started helping themselves to the slices of white, tender chicken flecked with dark green specks of tarragon, the hunks of crusty bread, and the salad. For a while, they were quiet, concentrating on the food. Then Fred set his plate down, stretched, and patted his stomach. "Delicious again, Dave."

David looked pleased. "Thanks, Dad."

Fred stood up. "Anyone up for a little stroll around the lake? There's a nice path that goes right along the bank."

"Sure!" Mom got to her feet and dusted off her shorts. "Are you coming, Bob?" she asked. Maddy's father had just stretched out flat on the sand with a towel over his eyes, but he reluctantly removed it and got up.

"I think I'm going swimming," David said.

"Maddy?" Fred asked, inviting her to join them for a stroll.

She glanced at David, who seemed to be unsuccessfully trying not to stare at her. "Um, I think I'll hang out here, Fred, thanks. Maybe I'll swim too." She leaned back on her elbows and smiled at the group.

"Okay. Let's go." Maddy watched as her parents and Fred crunched away down the beach and disappeared on a path through the woods. She and David were quiet. After the sound of footsteps faded away, Maddy tried to concentrate on stacking up a little pile of stones. David examined a mosquito bite on his toe. A black ant wandered onto the blanket and started trying to carry away a bread crumb. The quiet stretched out until Maddy felt it change into something else. She started feeling a little awkward, like she was overly aware of her hands, and she could tell David felt it too. All of a sudden she realized what it was. *We're alone.* It didn't really make sense—she had been alone with David for days at a time, but for some reason, this felt different. She could sense just how close to her he was sitting, and her skin tingled a little.

He stood up abruptly. "Let's swim."

"Okay," she answered, thankful for the break in the silence.

Without waiting for her, he took off his flip-flops and walked out onto the dock, where he stopped and stripped off his shirt. His broad shoulders were well muscled and deeply tanned, tapering to narrow hips. He turned around and stretched his arms overhead, making his pecs and abs ripple, and executed a perfect backward dive into the gray-green water. A moment later, his dark head appeared, gleaming on the surface of the water. He swam back and forth a few times and then flipped over onto his back. "Come on!" he called to her. "It's not that cold!"

"I'm not scared of cold water!" she called back.

"Then come on in! Or are you not as tough as you act?"

She couldn't let him get away with that. "Okay, Superboy, I'm coming!" She pulled her tank top off over her head, feeling a little like she was doing a striptease, even though she was wearing a swimsuit. She wiggled out of her jeans and undid her ponytail, raking her fingers through her hair. She flipped it back over her shoulders, where it hung, tickling the bare skin between her shoulder blades. She could tell David was watching her and it made her nervous. This was dumb. Why should she be nervous? It was just David.

He was treading water as she strode out onto the dock. The gray planks were smooth and hot under her bare feet. She stood at the end and looked down into the green depths. Sunlight filtered through the top of the water, turning it translucent. Below that, it was just dark. A spray of water splashed her feet and calves. "Stop!" she shrieked, retreating to the other side of the dock.

David grinned and splashed her again. "Come on, chicken girl!"

She stuck her tongue out at him, took a deep breath, and dove into the water. She gasped as she came to the surface. "It's freezing, you ass!"

David laughed. He turned a somersault and then swam away from her across the water. Maddy struck out after him, pulling at the water with her best summer swim-team strokes. Swimming in the lake felt very different from swimming in the chlorinated crystal-clear blue depths of the Bay Swim Club pool. For one thing, it felt very big. She couldn't help feeling a tiny bit nervous about the deep, dark water below her. She knew that there weren't any sharks or anything in a lake, but maybe . . . snakes? Immersed in her thoughts, she hadn't noticed David disappear from her line of vision. She stopped swimming and treaded water for a minute, looking around. Where was he? She couldn't see him anywhere. Suddenly, from under the water, something grabbed her ankles and pulled hard, forcing her head under the surface. She tried to scream but inhaled a mouthful of lake water instead. For one terrifying instant, she floundered under the water, still held around the ankles, choking on the water she had swallowed.

Then her ankles were released. Her head broke the surface and she gasped. David was beside her, his arm around her waist, supporting her as he held on to the dock with the other hand. Maddy sputtered a minute, catching her breath, clinging to his strong shoulders. "Thanks a lot!" she finally managed.

He looked abashed. "Sorry about that—I didn't mean for you to swallow water. You can get me back."

Suddenly, she was conscious of how close she was to him. She released her hold quickly and swam away. "I'm okay now!" she called back over her shoulder.

"You sure?" he called after her.

"I'm fine!" she said, breaststroking along the waterline. Now that she was more used to it, the contrast between the warm sun on her shoulders and the cool water felt good. She swam laps for a few minutes, plotting out a little friendly revenge. Some long strands of pondweed floating near the surface of the water close to the shore gave her an idea, even if it was a little silly.

She pulled up some of the slimy green weeds and twisted them into a cool, wet wad. Then, holding her weapon in one hand, she paddled back toward David. She was pretty near him when he saw her and said, "Hey. What's up?"

"This!" she yelled, and threw the pondweed. She scored a direct hit right on his forehead. He yelped and pawed the stuff off before dunking his head in the water to get rid of the sliminess.

He was laughing when he came up. "Oh, you're bad," he said. "Better run away." He tried to grab her around the waist but she slipped out of his hands and backstroked across the lake beyond his reach. "Bye!" She waved.

"Nice try!" he called and swam rapidly toward her, beating the dark water into white froth behind him. Maddy shrieked with pretend fright and paddled in a large circle. David snared her, this time successfully wrapping his arms around her. She felt a thrill of excitement at the touch of his smooth chest, deliciously warm under the cold water.

"Arrrrahh!" David attempted a kung fu yell and, lifting Maddy like she weighed nothing, threw her into the water. She shook her hair out of her face as she came up.

"You're in so much trouble, jerk!" she yelled, and flung herself onto his back, sticking there like a suction cup. They sank and David started swimming near the bottom of the pond, Maddy still hanging on to his shoulders.

All of the surface noises disappeared, leaving the two of them in cool green silence. The pondweed waved beneath them, and dark logs lay here and there, half buried in the underwater mud. Maddy felt like she and David had entered their own world for a moment— a bubble where no one existed but the two of them.

Then the spell was broken as David swam upward and they surfaced. "Woo-hoo!" Maddy gasped. "I had no idea I could hold my breath that long!"

"You just have to practice—Jeremy Olson and I used

to have contests in his basement in fourth grade. First one to black out was the loser."

Maddy laughed, still panting. She treaded water, holding on to his shoulder with one hand. "Sounds great." The words died on her lips as she suddenly realized how close their faces were—only inches away. Her eyes were drawn to his lips like magnets. Her hands grew numb and her face started tingling as she realized he was staring at her too.

What are you doing, Maddy? A little, sane voice in her head pushed through the haze in her mind. Excellent question. She ripped her eyes from David's face and, turning, swam slowly back toward the dock, which was now only a thin gray line above the water. David paddled by her side.

For a minute, neither spoke. Maddy cast a glance at David under her eyelashes. His face was pleasant as usual but told her nothing about what he was thinking. Then he turned to her. "Can I tell you something?" he asked.

"Sure," she said, watching the dock slowly grow larger in front of them.

"I was wrong about you."

Maddy blinked at the boldness of his words. "What?"

He turned his head as best he could while still swimming. "I mean it. When I first met you, I thought you were someone different than you are."

Maddy was almost afraid to ask. "What . . . what did you think I was?"

"Oh, I don't know—maybe a little snobby?"

She opened her mouth.

David rushed ahead. "Hey, that's not what I wanted to tell you. I was wrong, because it turns out that you're really a hell of a lot of fun. I know this isn't exactly the summer you'd hoped for. It wasn't my plan, either. But this summer is turning out fifty times better than I thought it would. Score one for changing plans!"

Warmth flooded Maddy's body as she took in his words. She felt buoyant, like she could just float across the lake instead of swimming. She grinned at David. "I can't disagree with you."

David pulled himself out onto the dock, but Maddy swam to the shore and waded in, wrinkling her nose at the feel of the muddy sand. Her parents and Fred had returned from their walk and were busily shaking out blankets and folding chairs. Maddy wrapped a towel around her shoulders. David came up behind her, panting a little and dripping.

Maddy picked up an armful of blankets and worked her feet into her flip-flops.

"Back to the grind tomorrow," she said to David with a mock sigh as they struggled toward the woods.

"Yeah, we can inhale bleach fumes together all day. I'm sure I have a few brain cells left that haven't been fried yet."

Maddy pulled a mournful face, but the truth was, as they all walked together toward their trucks, tired and sandy, she didn't really mind the thought of working on the tasting room with David. She actually couldn't think of anything else she'd rather do.

Chapter Fourteen

◆

Maddy sat with her parents in the living room that night after dinner. She had washed off in the outdoor shower stall after coming back from the lake, and the scent of citrus soap still lingered on her skin. Her stomach felt pleasantly full of her mother's penne with sun-dried tomatoes and fresh local broccoli. Idly wondering why it was that her parents had decided to start living without a TV, she dug a puzzle out of the closet. The box sported a sweeping photo of the Grand Canyon in an improbable shade of orange. She spread the pieces out on the shiny pine coffee table and sat down on the floor to sort them out.

The windows were open and the white lace curtains fluttered softly in the night breeze. Maddy's mother was curled up in a big soft armchair, reading under a pool of yellow lamplight. Dad had stretched out on the slouchy green velour sofa. He looked like he might fall asleep any minute. Maddy snapped two puzzle pieces.

Her mother looked up from her book and cleared her throat. "Maddy, honey."

"Yeah?"

She leaned forward. "Your dad and I were talking about your birthday and considering what you said last week." Maddy's heart leaped for a minute. Maybe they had changed their minds. "And while we haven't changed our minds about a trip to the city, we understand that you want to see your friends."

Maddy nodded. "I do, Mom."

"So we thought that you might want to invite Brian up to the vineyard for a birthday dinner here. That way we can still be together as a family."

Maddy considered the offer. It wasn't what she'd had in mind, but it was better than nothing. At least they were trying. "Thanks, guys. I think that would be great." Her mom relaxed visibly.

"I know this hasn't been your ideal summer, honey," she said. "But I want you to know just how much we appreciate all your hard work on the tasting room and around the place. You've done a really nice job."

"Thanks," Maddy said. "I'm going to go call Brian then, okay?"

Maddy's room was filled with the scent of honey-suckle from the night air. Her dad had installed some screens, so now she could keep her porch doors open without getting eaten alive by mosquitoes during the night. She didn't bother turning on the lights. Just enough light filtered in from the kitchen windows below. Maddy pulled on a pair of soft gray jersey shorts and a camisole and stretched out on her bed. She reached for her phone, ignoring the nervous feeling in her stomach. She and Brian still had talked only once since David had grabbed the phone, and it hadn't gone particularly well. It was weird calling and not knowing if Brian would be mad or not. Hopefully, this invite would just smooth everything over. He could come up here and they could pick up right where they'd left off. Maddy smiled at the thought and speed-dialed Brian's number.

"Hey, babe," he answered.

"Hi—how are you?" Maddy said.

"Great."

There was a moment's pause and then Maddy said, "What are you up to?"

"Nothing—just hanging out on the couch, watching the Giants. Chad's coming by—I think we might go over to Morgan's in a while. She's having some people over to hang out in her hot tub." He didn't *sound* angry.

"That'll be fun," Maddy said automatically. "Um, Brian?"

"Yeah?"

"So, you aren't still mad?" she asked carefully.

"About what?"

Maddy couldn't believe it. "You know, the last couple times we talked? And—" She didn't really want to remind him of the whole David incident if he barely remembered.

"Oh, whatever. I'd completely forgotten about that. It's no big deal," Brian said. Maddy could hear the roar of the television in the background. "Yes! Touchdown!" Brian yelled.

Maddy fell on her back and stared at the ceiling. Incredible. Here she was, obsessing for days, worrying he was mad at her, going over everything in her head a thousand times, and he wasn't even thinking about it! That was so typical.

Oblivious to Maddy's inner turmoil, Brian went on. "So, did you ask your parents about coming down for your birthday?"

Okay, apparently we're moving on. "I did," she replied, "and we had the worst fight. I was so mad—they actually wanted to take me to dinner and a movie with just them instead of letting me drive to see you."

"That's typical of them," Brian offered. "They're so lame."

Maddy felt a stab of defensiveness. She'd called her parents lame herself a million times, but for some reason, it seemed different when he did it. "Well, it turned out okay, actually. They said today that you could come up to the vineyard for my birthday instead!"

"Cool."

Maddy waited for a moment, but he didn't go on. "Cool? That's it? That's all you're going to say?"

"Yeah, well, it'll be great to see you, but obviously it's hard to get all worked up about a two-hour drive, followed by hanging out on a farm."

"Well, I think it could be fun," Maddy said quietly.

"Yeah, maybe. Anyway, what are you doing up there in No Man's Land?"

"Oh, we had a good time today. We all went up to this lake that Fred knew about—Fred's my dad's business partner—and had a picnic, and David and I swam. It was beautiful. There was a little beach and a dock. . . ." She trailed off.

Brian laughed. "Wow, swimming in a lake. I guess that guy's rubbing off on you, nature girl. What's next, volunteering for Greenpeace?"

Maddy sat up in bed. "It was fun! Look, you'll see when you come up here—it's actually really gorgeous. Wait until you see the room we're fixing up—it looks so different than when we started. It's all scrubbed and clean. We're getting ready to paint it now."

"You're getting me all turned on talking about scrubbing and painting," Brian scoffed. "I can't handle it."

"Stop. You don't get it. I'm not just talking about the work. It's just the whole *feel* of the place. . . ." She struggled to find the right words. "I mean, everyone's so much more relaxed—like, today, we watched six deer meet in the yard. Do you see what I mean?"

"No. What do deer have to do with being relaxed?"

"I don't know. I'm not sure what I'm talking about."

"Yeah, no kidding." They were quiet for a minute. Finally, Brian said, "Well, I think that's Chad at the door."

"Okay," she said. She felt tired all of a sudden. "Do you want to come up on Saturday or not?"

"Of course I do. I'll see you then, okay?"

"Yeah, okay. Bye."

"Bye, babe." He hung up. Maddy clicked her phone off and fell back on the bed, stretching her legs up against the wall. She was irritated and didn't know why. She really wanted Brian to understand, but for the first time he didn't seem to get her. The vineyard was turning out to be different than she'd thought. Maddy examined her tanned arms, which were starting to show muscle definition for the first time in her life. She had never been outdoors so constantly and, honestly, it felt good. Being surrounded by the grapevines, trees, and flowers of Napa all day, every day, felt satisfying—like eating a really great meal. She was surprised at herself, too. David wasn't the only one who hadn't realized Madeline Sinclaire was more than a pampered city girl.

Maddy crooked her arm over her eyes and relaxed into the pillows. *Maybe Brian will understand once he actually gets up here,* she comforted herself. As she lay in the darkness, spinning pleasant images of her and Brian frolicking in the stream at the bottom of the field, Maddy realized that the cricket on the porch had been singing his nightly song for a while now. *CHEEP, cheep, CHEEP, cheep.* She hadn't even noticed.

Chapter Fifteen

✦

The interior of the gray pickup was hot, but David had both windows rolled down and music blasting when Maddy climbed onto the passenger seat at noon on Wednesday. "Hi," he greeted her.

"Hi." Maddy buckled her seat belt and rested her elbow on the edge of the open window. She noticed his eyes lingering on her hair.

"I like that . . . um—hairdo," David said.

"Thanks," Maddy said, hiding a smile. She had spent several extra minutes that morning pulling her hair into a high, elegant chignon that showed off her neck and bare shoulders. David passed her a crumpled scrap of paper.

"Here are the directions. I think it's next to Jay's Ice Cream."

Maddy squinted at the smeary ballpoint pen scratchings. The tasting room had been scrubbed sparkling clean, so Maddy had convinced David that they should choose the furniture for it now, before they started painting. Even if they found the tables and chairs today, it would take a while for everything to be delivered. At first he had resisted, moaning that he *hated* shopping, but she'd won after pointing out that it was going to be pretty tough for the winery guests to relax in an empty room. So they were headed for the best furniture showroom in Napa. In honor of escaping to the nearest semi-large town, Maddy was wearing a lavender Marc Jacobs shift dress and silver hoop earrings. After weeks of shorts, jeans, and T-shirts, if felt good to be dressed up.

Maddy looked up from the directions, noticing what was pumping through the stereo speakers. "Is that *salsa* you have on?" she asked incredulously.

"Oh, um, yeah." He glanced sideways at her and quickly turned it off.

"Wait, don't," she insisted. "I like it."

"You do?" Now it was his turn to sound incredulous.

"Yeah. It's good driving music." There was a long pause, as if David was trying to figure out if she was serious or not. Finally, a big grin split his face.

"Okay." He turned the stereo back on. "You've surprised me once more, Maddy-Mae," he said.

Maddy bit her lower lip and smiled. "Left on Redbrick," she murmured.

◆ ◆ ◆

David started fidgeting the moment they walked into the showroom. The interior was all sleek dark surfaces and cool polished marble. Sun filtered through the sky-lights, casting shadows on the tables, and there were chairs scattered in tasteful groups around the cavernous space.

"Okay, this was great," David announced, turning back toward the big glass doors. "I'm glad we did this and—" Maddy grabbed his arm, trying not to laugh.

"Come on, I'm sure you can handle more than two minutes of shopping. Get a grip!" she instructed. "Here, I made a list of the things we'll need." She took it out of her Kooba bag.

"Four small round tables, sixteen chairs," he read, "four armchairs, two love seats, two low tables, one high narrow table—oh my God, I think I'm breaking out in hives."

"Can I help you?" A bald man stood in front of them. He was slender and neat, with cuff links and pre-cisely pressed slacks. He wore geometric black-framed glasses and a skinny maroon tie.

"Yeah, thanks," David said. He thrust the list at the

man. "We'll just take these things in, um . . ." He turned to Maddy. "Is brown okay?"

Maddy wrinkled her nose at him. "We're not at In-N-Out Burger," she teased. She turned to the salesman. "Would you mind showing us around a little? We're interested in clean, classic, elegant lines, nothing fussy. Also, I want everything to be comfortable—that's important."

The little man looked newly respectful. "Of course, ma'am. My name is Harrison. If you'll come this way, I think you might be interested in the Verona line." He led them toward a table and a grouping of chairs near the front. "These are walnut, with maple inlay. They were featured in *Town & Country* last April. Are you and your husband looking to furnish your living room or dining room?"

Maddy widened her eyes at David behind Harrison's back and mouthed, "Husband?" He winked back.

"Yes, these look great, Harrison," he said. "My wife and I are furnishing both our living room and our dining room. We hardly have any furniture at all."

"Ah," Harrison chuckled gently. "Newlyweds?"

Maddy was trying to keep a hold of her giggles, but her face was flaming and her eyes were brimming with tears from the effort. She pretended to cough into her elbow. "Well, *dear*," she said to David, "I'd like to look around a little, if you don't mind."

"Not at all, sweetie." David's eyes were sparkling

mischievously. He draped an arm around Maddy's shoulders and pulled her against him, ignoring the startled little squawk she let out. "What about this little ensemble?" He pointed to a sofa and easy chairs upholstered in prickly yellow silk.

Maddy shot a quick glance at Harrison, who was watching benevolently. She could practically read his mind: *What a nice young couple.* She tried to refocus her attention away from the sensation of David's arm around her to the furniture. She cleared her throat. "I'm not sure that will go with our look, *Davey*. But this would be perfect." She patted a sleek brown leather sofa and turned to Harrison, who was standing ready with a pad of paper and a pen. "We'll take this."

"Of course." He made a note on his pad. "Will you be needing tables as well, Mrs. . . . ?"

"Uh, Sinclaire—ah, *Ms.* Sinclaire," Maddy replied quickly. Out of the corner of her eye, she could see David grinning broadly. "I'm keeping my maiden name." She tried for a convincingly nonchalant tone. David snorted and she dug her elbow into his ribs.

Harrison trotted after them as they perused the rest of the store, selecting little tables, easy chairs, straight chairs, and one gorgeous long oak table to place against the wall. Maddy could just picture bottles crowding its surface, wineglasses lined up in sparkling rows, and big bowls of grapes at either end.

"Wow," she said to David finally, "we've been here for over an hour and look—you still haven't broken out in hives." She held his muscular arm up to the light and pretended to examine his skin.

"I know—it's practically a miracle. But now I have another serious medical problem."

"What?" Maddy asked.

"I'm dying of starvation." He clutched his stomach dramatically.

Maddy laughed. "Okay, you're right. I think we have everything anyway. Let's get out of here."

Harrison rang them up and promised delivery in three weeks. He waved them out the door, looking extremely pleased. "He should," David said when Maddy mentioned this. "We're probably the best customers he's had all summer."

In the parking lot, they both slipped on sunglasses to fight against the blasting Napa sun. "So," Maddy said, wiggling her shoulders against the pickup seat and cranking down her window. "Where should we eat?"

"Umm . . ." David thought as they cruised down the two-lane road. Puffy white clouds skated across the azure sky, and the scent of hot grasses blew in through the two open windows.

"Aaaoohhh!" Maddy suddenly yelled, sticking her head out the window. She dropped back into the passenger seat. "Sorry. I just had to do that for a second. What a gorgeous day!"

"Nice Tarzan yell," David complimented her. "I think the last time I heard one that good, my buddy Rich was doing a cannonball off some cliffs on the coast."

"Thanks—wait!" Maddy suddenly shrieked, grabbing David's arm. "Turn back, turn back!"

"What is it?" He did a U-turn in the middle of the road.

"Pull in there! That's exactly what I want for lunch." She pointed to a little wooden shack by the side of the road. A giant barbecue cooker was sitting in the middle of the parking lot, smoke pouring from its opening. Watched avidly by two dogs, an old guy in a stained white apron was poking the meat with a long metal fork. David parked right next to a sign reading PORK RIBS: HALF RACK $3, FULL RACK $5 W/2 SIDES.

✦ ✦ ✦

Twenty minutes later, David heaved a long sigh as he gazed down at the heap of shining bones in front of him. "You were absolutely right," he said, wiggling around until he was lying flat on the bench of the picnic table at the side of the parking lot. "That was the world's best lunch. I've never had barbecue sauce that good."

"Mmmff," Maddy agreed, gnawing at a rib. Her fingers were sticky and she knew she probably had a smear of sauce on her face somewhere, but she didn't care. All she felt was happiness—she'd had a great meal, a successful morning, and she could feel the warm sun as she reclined at this old picnic table with David. He suddenly popped back up.

"What is it with you?" he exclaimed, staring right at her.

"Do I have more sauce on my face?" Maddy asked, reaching for her napkin.

"I'm not talking about sauce," he said. "I'm talking about you. You keep confusing the hell out of me. How many girls do you know who can go from picking out fancy furniture to eating pork in an old parking lot and be perfectly comfortable with both?"

Maddy shrugged. "I love ribs. Anyway, don't you think this kind is a hundred times better than the stuff you get in most restaurants?"

"Yeah, of course I do. I just wasn't expecting *you* to think that too."

Maddy leaned forward and slurped her iced tea without picking up the Styrofoam cup. Her hands were still covered with sauce. "Actually," she admitted, "I'm kind of surprised at me too. I mean, I really do love ribs. But you're right. It usually wouldn't occur to me to just pull over somewhere like we did. I don't know what it is—the place looked good and I just *felt* like it, ya know?"

David was staring at her thoughtfully. "Yeah," he said, piling their trash up in the middle of the table. "I feel the same way—it must be something in the air up here."

Whatever it is, Maddy thought, scrubbing at her hands with a napkin, *I like it.*

Chapter Sixteen

◆

I'm so glad Dad agreed to go with the cream color," Maddy said, keeping her eyes on the strip she was carefully painting by the door. "Can you believe he actually wanted *maroon*?"

"If you want total honesty," David replied, "I thought maroon would be fine, but now that we've started, I can see what you mean. The maroon would've been really dark."

"Right. When you have a small space, even with these high ceilings, you want to open it up with a light color."

They had been painting most of the morning. The tasting room was explosively hot, and the breeze through the open double doors didn't help much.

Maddy had been combating the problem by occasionally dunking a bandanna in water and then tying it around her head. She felt like she had already sweated off about two pounds in water weight.

A trickle of sweat ran past her forehead, stinging her eye. She straightened up carefully and tried to wipe it away with her forearm, since that was one of the only parts of her body not sprinkled with paint. She cast a surreptitious glance at David. He had taken off his shirt long ago, pointing out that it wasn't very comfortable wearing a piece of sweat-soaked cotton all day in ninety-five-degree heat. His tanned back was smooth and muscular above the waist of his baggy shorts. He was carefully painting the walls with a long roller. As a result, a gentle shower of paint had covered his curls, face, arms, and shoulders. He looked like he'd been dusted with powdered sugar.

"See—this is why we make a good team," David said, spreading wider and wider swathes of bright cream onto the dingy plaster. "If this was all left to me, it'd be maroon with whatever furniture I saw first at Target."

Maddy knee-walked over to a new section. David's words sent a warm feeling all through her body. "You'd be fine," she told him. "But maybe there is something to what they say about a woman's touch. . . ." She tied up the bottom of her old tank top, exposing her sweat-beaded stomach.

David set his roller carefully in a tray of paint and turned around to wipe his face with his T-shirt, which he'd flung over the back of a chair. A wicked thought occurred to Maddy. She rose and padded silently across the floor toward him. "Then there's this sort of touch too," she said to his back, and lifting her wide brush, she painted a long cream streak between his bare, sweaty shoulder blades.

"Hey!" he yelped, swinging around at the touch of the brush. He swiped at his back and came up with a palmful of wet paint. Giggling uncontrollably, Maddy retreated to the other side of the room.

"I'm sorry," she sputtered. "It must be the paint fumes. . . ."

"Riiight," David said, advancing slowly across the floor, roller in hand. "I'm starting to feel a little light-headed too. . . ." He raised the roller and charged at her as she shrieked and retreated behind a ladder, laughing so hard tears spurted from her eyes. For a moment, they feinted right and left, and then Maddy lunged toward the door. "Don't even think about it!" David yelled, tossing aside a chair and running after her.

Maddy burst outside and flew across the soft green grass, splashed through the stream, and came to a halt in the field on the other side. She turned around, grinning. David was standing on the other side of the stream, roller still clutched in his hand. "Come here, little Maddy-Mae," he wheedled, stepping into the stream.

"Stop. Stop!" she cried, holding up her hands. "Truce! I just couldn't resist."

"Okay," he said. "I'll forgive you if you come over here and get this paint off my back—here, I'll even put the roller down." He ostentatiously placed it several feet away. Maddy stepped back across the stream gingerly. She searched around for something to wipe his back off with.

"Wait, hold on," she said, and dashed back into the tasting room. She returned with his discarded T-shirt. David was sitting on the grassy stream bank. "Here, turn around." She dipped the shirt into the icy water and wrung it out. She knelt next to him and scrubbed, watching his skin turn red. They were quiet as she worked, and suddenly Maddy felt guilty—as if they were doing something wrong. *But we aren't,* she told herself. It wasn't like she was cheating on Brian or anything. They were just goofing around—and it wasn't even like they had *chosen* to spend all this time together. They had to. Maddy was startled out of her reverie by the sound of a horse's heavy breathing. She looked up.

Rain brushed her sun-kissed hair out of her face as she smiled down at them. "Hey, guys. I had a break in my schedule and thought I'd see if anyone wanted to go for a ride."

Maddy noticed that, although she seemed to be

speaking to both of them, Rain hadn't actually looked at her once. She quickly glanced over at David, trying to gauge whether he was excited or annoyed by the interruption. His face was frustratingly blank.

"Hi, Rain." David squinted up at her.

"Looks like you've had quite a morning," Rain continued, her offer going ignored.

This perked David up. "You could say that," he laughed, smirking at Maddy.

Maddy set the wet shirt aside. "Well, the paint's all gone," she said. She lay back on the cool grass and put her hands behind her head, staring up at the sky. A pale daytime moon was just visible overhead.

"Wow, thank you so much for cleaning up your own mess." David grinned.

"So, anyone up for a ride?" Rain hopped down from the commanding gray horse. She reached into the saddlebag and took out a brush, giving the horse's mane a few strokes.

David looked down at Maddy. She shrugged her shoulders, the warm grass tickling her arms.

"Actually, we've got a lot of work to finish up today. Maybe another time," David offered without much enthusiasm. Rain looked surprised.

"Oh, well, okay. I should probably be getting back anyway." She gracefully swung herself back up into her saddle. "Bye."

As Rain rode off, David sank back next to Maddy. He stretched his arms overhead.

Maddy turned to face him. "No riding with Rain for you today?"

"No," David said, keeping his eyes glued to a passing cloud. He paused, as if unsure whether or not to continue. "She's a little superior all the time, you know? Like anyone who's not just like her is beneath her somehow?"

Maddy turned away so David wouldn't see how broadly she was smiling. "Yeah," she replied. "I got that vibe too."

They chatted about the paint job for a while, and then David mentioned that the Robertsons, who had hosted the pre-harvest dinner, had asked him to cook for one of their upcoming parties.

"What are you going to make?" Maddy asked idly, gazing at a cloud that looked like a mushroom.

David nibbled on a blade of grass. "I think maybe lamb ragout. People usually get a kick out of that, and everyone likes it." His voice was slow and sleepy. They lay in comfortable silence for a few minutes, drinking in the sunshine like warm honey, letting the dragonflies buzz over their inert figures.

Then Maddy spoke. "I think I'd like to learn to cook sometime." The words seemed to bubble out of her of their own accord. For a moment, she felt surprised. *You would?* "Yeah, I would," she said aloud.

David removed the blade of grass from his mouth and turned his head toward her. Maddy turned hers too, and they looked at each other from only a few inches away. Maddy realized for the first time how close they were lying. She could almost feel his breath on her cheek. "Maybe . . . you could give me some lessons."

"Yeah . . . sure." For a moment, they just stared at each other, both smiling. "What, um, do you want to learn to make?"

Maddy considered this. "I don't know—a soufflé?"

"Do you like soufflé?"

"I don't know." She laughed. "I've never eaten one. You just always hear about people trying to cook soufflés and messing them up."

He laughed too. "We should do something easy, so it'll actually be edible at the end. Okay, how about this—what are your favorite flavors? Like, mine are lime, mango, anything roasted, and anything battered and fried."

"Hmm." Maddy pondered. "I like that question. Maybe . . . chocolate, raspberry, coffee, and—this might sound kind of weird—but I really love smelly cheese. Like the kind with mold that's supposed to be there?"

"Yeah, blue cheese. I love that too. It's really strong, though."

"I know. Ever since I was little, I've always liked strong, salty things—even sardines!"

"Wow," David said approvingly. "My grandma likes sardines."

Maddy sighed. "That's good. I thought I was the only person in the world, but I'm glad there's an old lady out there who likes them too."

"Um-hm."

She glanced over at David. He was lying with his hands crossed on his chest, and his eyes were closed. As she watched, he took a long, slow breath and then another. "Are you falling asleep?" she asked, propping herself up on one elbow.

"Huh-mm."

Maddy curled up and tucked her hands under her cheek. The grass was soft and the breeze felt lovely on her face. She closed her eyes too and, listening to David's regular breathing beside her, fell asleep.

Chapter Seventeen

✦

Mads," Maddy's father said, coming into the kitchen the next morning while Maddy was sitting half awake over her bagel and cream cheese.

"What?" She didn't care how long she'd been in Napa—she still didn't like 7 A.M. Her hair was tied up in a messy ponytail and she was wearing a DANCE THE NIGHT AWAY PROM 2008 T-shirt and a pair of boxers with teddy bears on them.

Her dad poured himself a cup of coffee and, leaning an elbow on the counter, downed half of it in two gulps. "Mom and I want you to have a break on your birthday—and David, too. So take Saturday off, okay? No working—don't even try to sneak in a little painting. And tell David the same goes for him."

"Aw, thanks, Daddy." Maddy rose from the table and gave him a hug. He squeezed her back and then headed for the porch. At the door, he turned.

"Oh, and we're going to have a birthday dinner, here at the vineyard, for everyone."

"That'll be great. Brian will love it."

"Well, I hope *you* love it. It's not his birthday."

Maddy rolled her eyes. "I know, Dad." He waved and Maddy heard him clattering down the porch steps.

Maddy stuffed the rest of the bagel into her mouth and, after a quick glance around, took a swig of orange juice straight from the carton. Saturday would be great, she decided as she climbed the stairs for her shower. A whole day with Brian. The idea *sounded* good, but she didn't feel that thrill of excitement in the pit of her stomach when she thought about it. She just felt sort of . . . *eh*. Napa had really taken over her brain, she mused, staring idly into the bathroom mirror. She was getting an excellent tan, though.

✦ ✦ ✦

"Guess what?" Maddy said to David a couple hours later. All around them, crystal sparkled on glass shelves of Standish & Sons—the biggest glassware dealer in wine country—dramatically displayed against dark blue walls. David hadn't even moaned about shopping when Maddy told him they needed to go pick out wineglasses for the tasting room.

"What?" He poured a little Perrier into a wineglass they were testing. A dozen different glasses were spread out on the sleek black table in front of them, all shapes, heights, and sizes. "Look, this is what you're supposed to do with wine," he said. He stuck his nose into the glass as far as it would go and inhaled deeply. "Ah, what a bouquet," he murmured in a fake French accent.

"Mmm, *le scent du Perrier*," Maddy teased. She poured some water into another glass and held it up. "This one is so sparkly." She admired the sparks of blue, orange, and purple shooting from the crystal as she twisted it in a beam of sunlight. "I like the shape of these big ones. What do you think?"

David glanced over at the huge balloon glass. "I could take a bath in that one. How about this?" He held up a smaller, more slender version.

"Okay," Maddy said doubtfully. "A little *boring*. How about something more edgy? Anyway, don't you want to know what I was going to say?"

"Yeah, what?" He set the glass down and turned to her.

"Well, my dad told me to tell you that we get my birthday off on Saturday." Maddy grinned, anticipating his reaction.

"Woo-hoo!" he hooted. "Wow! No work for an entire

day!" He gave her a little hug, which left her breathless. "I'm actually really excited."

Maddy grinned, her fingertips tingling a little. "Me too. We're such nerds—all worked up about one day with no work."

"I know."

They kept grinning at each other. Maddy had to force herself not to hug him again.

"Oh, and I almost forgot," she went on once she had regained control of her hands, "there's going to be a birthday dinner, too."

"Cool! Who's cooking?" David took a sip of Perrier out of a champagne flute that had somehow wound up on their table.

Maddy set aside eight glasses she didn't like and lined up four possibilities in front of them. "I don't know— probably my mom. I think it'll be just us and your dad and my parents and—" She shut her mouth abruptly. For some reason, she didn't feel like mentioning that Brian would be there also. She held up her favorite wineglass instead. "Okay, what do you think of this one? It's gorgeous, perfectly proportioned, and not horribly expensive."

David nodded. "Good. Let's do it. Hey, I could give your mom some suggestions for your birthday dinner. I have this amazing torte recipe we could do with fresh raspberries. And I know the best place to set up the outdoor table, too." He led the way to the counter at the front, chattering about plans, while a wave of guilt swept over Maddy.

Back in the truck, she made her decision. It was wrong not to mention that Brian was coming to visit, though wrong to David or Brian, she didn't know. David clicked on the radio and made a face as country music blared from the speakers. "Wow, my dad must have been driving last," he shouted over the twanging guitars. Keeping one eye on the road, he punched in an oldies station. "I think this is the best we're going to get out here," he said, tapping in time to "Respect."

Maddy suddenly reached over and clicked Aretha off in the middle of *"find out what it means to me."* David glanced over.

"What, you don't like Aretha?"

"No, I love Aretha. Um, hey!" She tapped her cheek as if something had just occurred to her. "I totally forgot to tell you—Brian's coming for a visit . . . on Saturday." She faltered a little at the end and watched his face nervously.

For an infinitesimal moment, his hands tightened on the steering wheel hard enough to turn his knuckles white. Then he relaxed them with what seemed like a conscious effort. "Oh, yeah?" he said.

"Yeah."

The silence in the truck felt like it was expanding,

pressing against the windshield, bulging into the back of the cab. They both stared straight ahead for a few miles. *This is stupid,* Maddy thought. She spoke aloud. "So, won't it be exciting when they deliver the furniture?"

David stared straight ahead as he drove. "Yeah." His voice sounded hollow. More silence. Maddy was starting to feel a little pissed. He'd known all along that she had a boyfriend. They'd definitely had a great time working and hanging out together, but she needed to focus on Brian for a while now. It had been so long since they'd seen each other, and judging from their last phone call, they were in desperate need of quality time. It didn't take a rocket scientist to figure out that David was a little jealous. *Well,* she thought, *he's just going to have to deal with it.*

Chapter Eighteen

◆

From her perch on the old wooden porch swing on Saturday afternoon, Maddy could hear the purr of Brian's XTerra long before she actually saw it. She felt her pulse increase immediately but forced herself to sit still, gently pushing the swing back and forth with one bare toe. The sun was ferociously hot, but Maddy had found that if she didn't move too much and stayed in the shade, she could manage not to sweat through a new shirt every half hour she spent outside. The vineyard was very quiet, but she could hear all the sounds around her distinctly: Brian's motor, the *squee-squee* of the swing chains, and the faint ocean-wave rustle of the wind in the tops of the trees.

The yellow SUV swung into view, Fall Out Boy

blasting on the stereo. Through the windshield, Maddy could see Brian's tousled dark head and familiar Oakleys. He pulled up next to the Sinclaires' red pickup and killed the motor. Her first instinct was to leap up and call to him, but something kept her sitting quietly, hidden in the shadowy corner of the porch. For a long moment, he just sat in the driver's seat, tapping his fingers on the steering wheel, not moving. Then, just when Maddy was wondering why he wasn't getting out of the car, his door swung open. She could see that he was wearing his favorite crisp white cotton button-down, artfully opened to reveal a Calvin Klein tank undershirt. His jeans were dark-washed and perfectly frayed.

He stood by the car door, bouncing his keys in his hand. He looked like he was listening to the quiet also. She silenced the porch swing and sat still. Brian did a double take as he took in Bob's falling-apart truck. Maddy bit back a smile. The truck *was* a little startling; its bumper looked like it might come off at any moment. He stared at the house for a long moment, his face incredulous. Then he crunched toward the porch.

"Hey!" Maddy finally stood up. Brian jumped.

"Whoa, hey! Hi, babe. You startled me."

"Sorry." She ran down the steps to hug him. Despite all the weirdness on the phone, she was ridiculously glad to see him. "I'm so happy you're here!"

"Yeah, me too," he said, enfolding her in his arms.

Maddy wrapped her arms around his waist and leaned her head into his chest, waiting for that spark she always felt whenever he was around. But Brian was a little sweaty and sticky from being in the car.

He slapped his neck. They both looked at his hand as he drew it away. Smashed in the palm was a monster mosquito in a splatter of blood. Not the most romantic beginning to a date, but it didn't matter. Brian gave her another squeeze and then looked at her appraisingly. Something in his gaze made Maddy wonder if she should have blow-dried her hair and put on something other than jeans and a white tank top. He dropped his arms. "Got anything cold to drink?" he asked. "It's boiling out."

"Oh, yeah! I'm sorry, let's go around back. Then I can give you the tour."

"Great." He started following her, still staring at the house. "How do you all fit in this place?"

"Oh, it's not bad! It's actually bigger than it looks outside. I have my own room." She realized how that sounded. "Not that I *wouldn't* have my own room, I mean. I was just saying. . . ." She trailed off. She realized she didn't have the slightest idea what she was saying.

Brian was staring at her, his mouth slightly open.

"Anyway, the house is really cute inside," she continued nervously, unable to stem the flow of words. "And I have a porch." She pointed up to her balcony. "It's really great," she finished lamely. He was still staring.

"Good to know," he said finally. "Do you have an outhouse, too?"

"No, we actually have indoor plumbing, if you can believe that, and electricity, too. It's a really high-tech place," Maddy replied lightly.

"Wow. Now I *am* impressed."

Maddy smiled at Brian and took his arm but she felt more uncomfortable than she was letting on. It wasn't that he was teasing her about the vineyard—she had made fun of it plenty herself. It was something in the way he was acting. He seemed kind of ill at ease for some reason—not at all his usual imperturbable smooth self.

The sight of the backyard restored her equilibrium a little. The porch, with its overgrown trellises on either end, ivy hanging off the roof, and comfy rattan furniture, looked so cool and inviting. The grapevines lined the yard on three sides, dropping little grape clusters over the lawn like gifts. She turned to Brian expectantly. He was digging his phone out of his pocket. "This is the back," she declared.

He looked up. "Chad texted me. What did you say?"

Maddy struggled to control her annoyance. He'd only been here five minutes and he was already checking his messages? Plus, he wasn't even paying attention to the place. "I said, this is the backyard. See? Those are the grapevines there." She pointed.

"Oh, yeah. Cool," Brian managed.

Maddy gave up. "There's some mint iced tea in the kitchen," she said, opening the screen door. She sort of wished he would just stay on the porch, but he followed her in. He glanced around casually, taking in the simple kitchen with its bright yellow walls and wood floor, before leaning an elbow on the counter. Maddy bustled around getting out jelly glasses and the big frosty glass pitcher of tea. She loaded it all onto a tray and backed slowly out the screen door.

Brian flung himself onto one of the old rattan chairs and hooked a footstool over with a leg. Maddy handed him a glass and sat down on the top porch step, facing sideways, her back against the railing. Normally, she would have sat in his lap, but it was just too hot.

Brian drained his tea glass in three swallows and set it down with a deep sigh. Maddy put hers down too. She was remembering the junior prom just a few months ago. When he had seen her, posed at the top of the swirling marble staircase in the foyer of the Mandarin Oriental Hotel, clad in a shimmering red Versace gown, his mouth had dropped open. He couldn't stop staring at her. They all drank smuggled-in vodka tonics and danced until Morgan twisted her ankle in the middle of the dance floor and they had to carry her into the limo. All night, Maddy had felt Brian's gaze on her, and he constantly touched her hair or her neck. She'd felt like a princess. Now Maddy glanced at her boyfriend, who was fishing something out of his glass with his little finger. She didn't know why the prom memory had sprung up. Maybe it was because she felt so different from that girl in the red gown. It was like Brian had been plucked from her old city life and plopped down here on the porch, in her new Napa life. He still looked the same, but, looking down at her rolled-up jeans and earth-stained bare feet, she realized that she didn't.

Brian shifted a little in his chair. "So," he said. Maddy looked up eagerly at the sound of his voice. "As I was driving around looking for this place, totally lost, hoping I wouldn't run into the Toothless Hillbilly and *do-do dee-do-dee-do-dee*"—he mimicked the banjo tune from *Deliverance*—"I swear I drove past this store with the sign 'Live Bait and Video Rental.' Is that some kind of joke up here or something?"

"No, it's for real," Maddy explained. "Isn't that hilarious?"

"Yeah, I was cracking up."

Maddy gave a little laugh but it sounded forced, even to her own ears.

Brian leaned back in his chair and cracked his knuckles. "Where are your parents?" He grinned devilishly.

She grinned back. "They're out. They had to go to town to get some parts for the tractor. Fred's repairing some staking down in the right field, and David is . . .

actually, I don't know what he's doing."

A zing of tension floated through the air. Brian sat up in his chair slightly. "Oh, yeah, David. I forgot about that guy." His voice was casual. "Where's he from? Here?"

"Um, yeah. Well, for part of the year. The rest of the time he goes to Westside Public. I think he lives with his aunt and uncle in the city during the school year." Maddy focused on gathering their glasses on the tray. Her heart was beating fast, but she didn't know why. Nothing about David was a secret—he was just David. Brian was the important guy in her life, and he was right here in front of her. She took heart at this thought and looked up at her boyfriend with a genuine smile.

"Oh, yeah, Westside?" Brain snorted. "What's his dad do? Is he a garbage man or something?"

"No!" The vehemence of the word surprised them both. Maddy lowered her voice with an effort. "He's my dad's business partner, remember? Why are you being like this?"

"Sorry," he muttered. "I forgot about that. Look, come here, okay? I've been missing you."

She took a deep breath. "Whatever, forget it. Let's just enjoy the day, okay?"

He gave her a sexy smile. "Definitely." He held out his hand in truce. When she took it, he reached out and grabbed her waist, pulling her down on top of him.

She shrieked playfully and wiggled around so that she was facing him. His sharp blue eyes sparkled at her from his sunburned face.

"I missed you too," she said.

"Mmm." He massaged the backs of her thighs through her jeans and then slid his hands up until they were just below her butt. She closed her eyes. Their lips met, and then his tongue slid into her mouth. She drew back. She usually thought the tongue maneuver was pretty hot, but today, she just didn't feel like it. Maddy awkwardly disentangled herself and struggled up from his lap. What was the matter with her? Here was Brian, at the vineyard. They were going to make out a little— what was wrong with that? She didn't know, and that bothered her. Slightly breathless, she got to her feet and smoothed back her hair with both hands. Brian looked disappointed. "Come back here," he said, motioning to his lap.

"Don't you want a tour? I can show you the room I've been working on. It's in an old barn." Brian sighed and got up.

Maddy slipped on her Havaianas and led him to the path through the vines that started at the bottom of the lawn. She glanced over at Brian. His face was patchy and flushed from their brief make-out session and he looked pretty annoyed. She turned away. Whatever. She just wasn't in the mood right now. "We can take this down to the bottom of the vineyard, where there's an awesome stream. And then we can finish with the tasting room." She felt a little twinge of excitement. It *was* sort of amazing that she actually lived here.

"Hunh," Brian grunted behind her.

Still air, thick with the smell of mulch and soil and leaves, closed around them as they brushed between the rows of trellises. Maddy made herself be quiet as they walked single file down the path. She wanted to see if Brian would say anything. A few moments passed. He was silent behind her. She turned around. He was gazing at his cell phone. "Are you checking your messages again?" she asked incredulously.

"Yeah, sorry," he said, not looking up. "It's Chad—everyone's going to Tangerine tonight. I forgot to tell him I was coming up here. He wanted to know if I wanted to come over to his place first." He typed something rapidly on the keypad without breaking stride.

Maddy felt herself getting angry. *He could at least pretend to be interested,* she thought. *He's driven all the way up here.* She continued stewing as they wandered down the path but then exhaled audibly and tried to talk herself back into a better frame of mind. *You thought the vineyard was pretty boring too when you first came up here,* she reminded herself. *Brian just hasn't seen the cool parts yet. When he gets more used to the place, he'll see what you see.*

At the end of the field, the vines stopped and the

path widened. The meadow, the stream, and the shed were spread out before them like objects in a painting. "Isn't this gorgeous?" Maddy said hopefully.

"Yeah. So, what's up with tonight?" Brian asked.

She struggled to keep the wounded expression from her face as she answered. "It's just going to be a dinner here with my parents and David and Fred. Mom said it's a surprise. I think she's cooking something, or maybe Dad is. They've been whispering about it the last couple of days. I told her the only thing I absolutely had to have was something with chocolate and raspberries."

"Why's Crunchy coming?"

Maddy shot Brian a dirty look. "Why are you being so obnoxious? He's coming because he lives here."

"Where?"

"Here! Right over there." She pointed to the roof of the little white cottage, visible across the field. "He and Fred live in that house."

"They live *there*? What are they, white trash?"

Maddy stopped short and whipped around. Her face was hot with anger. "Why are you being such a total snob? I can't believe you," she fired at him.

Brian fell back a step and held up his hands. "Whoa— don't get all worked up." He flashed his disarming smile. "I was just kidding. Anyway, stop looking so cute or I'm going to have to . . ." He reached for her, but Maddy turned and strode rapidly to the banks of the stream.

The sight of the clear, golden water tumbling over the slick gray stones soothed her. She took a deep breath. "This is my favorite thinking place out here," she told Brian calmly. "Every day after we're done working, I come out here and sit on this big rock and relax. Isn't it peaceful? And you can see deer in the evening too."

"Cool."

Maddy climbed onto the rock and plunged her hot, dusty feet into the water. "Come on, Brian—it's nice and cold!"

He stood on the bank, looking a little hot and over-dressed in his long-sleeved shirt and dark jeans. "Look at you, hippie chick. What are you doing?" he said, not moving.

"I'm cooling off my feet. Come and sit next to me."

"I'm fine." It was obvious he wasn't going to put his feet in and that he wasn't interested in the stream. It was time to expedite the tour. She climbed off the big rock.

"Okay, well, the room I've been working on is over here."

"Great," he said unenthusiastically.

The little red building in front of them almost glowed in the slanting sunlight, which glinted on the tin roof. Dad hadn't been down here with the weed-whacker yet, so the long grasses lay in dry yellow swathes speckled with purple wildflowers around the foundation. Maddy unlatched and heaved open the big doors. The cream-painted walls glowed in the light-filled room. They had left the floors natural, but the planks were almost white from scrubbing. The rollers, paintbrushes, tarps, and paint cans were piled in a corner. The furniture and rug still hadn't arrived, so their footsteps echoed in the bareness. On an old table lay a big bunch of lavender Maddy had picked yesterday in an attempt to cover the paint smell.

"Wow!" Brian said in a goofy voice as they entered. "What time is the organic vegan yoga class?"

Maddy tried not to let her face show how much the comment wounded her. "I've been working really hard. David and I have been out here every day for like a month."

"I'm just teasing you, Mad! You've really lost your sense of humor since coming out here. I guess country living just sucked it all right out of you." Brian sat down on a barrel and took off one of his Reefs to examine his foot. "I've got a cut on my toe—I think I stepped on something." He looked up. "You mind if we head back to the house?"

Maddy sighed. "Sure. I'll find you a Band-Aid." She took one last look around the empty, silent room with the dust motes floating in the beams of sunlight and rolled the big doors shut with a rumbling thud.

As she followed Brian up the path to the house, she chewed over his comment about the vegan yoga class.

Something was off. After a minute, it came to her: Just a few months ago, that was exactly the kind of comment she would have made herself, or at least laughed at. Now she thought it was obnoxious and ignorant. The sinking feeling that had been growing in her chest all afternoon suddenly felt worse. She shook her head. *Look, Maddy,* she told herself, *you've wanted to see Brian all summer—obsessed about it, actually. Now he's here and it's a gorgeous day and you're together. So just stop overanalyzing everything and enjoy the time you have.*

Even as she psyched herself up, she knew that making this visit fun would be an uphill battle.

Chapter Nineteen

✦

Maddy! Come on, we're ready," Maddy's mother called from downstairs.

"Okay, coming!" Maddy examined herself carefully in the full-length mirror in her parents' room. Her long, strapless white cotton sundress had a full, gathered skirt and a tight empire bodice. It just brushed her ankles and showed off her golden tan. She had twisted her hair up into a casual knot at the back of her head. A chunky enamel bracelet in red and blue was her only jewelry.

There was a tap on the door frame. She turned around.

"Hey, babe," Brian said.

"Hi."

He had put on a blue button-down shirt and wet his hair down under the faucet. A leftover water droplet hung at his temple. He looked sexy as always.

"You look great," he said, coming into the room.

"Thanks."

"I brought your birthday present."

Her heart lifted. Maybe everything was going to be okay after all. "What is it?" She sat down on the edge of the bed.

He sat down next to her and took a box out of his pocket. He smelled like Davidoff Cool Water and hair gel.

Maddy looked into his face. "You're so sweet, babe," she said. "You didn't even ask me what I wanted!"

"I know. I didn't have to. Anyway, open it."

Carefully, she pried open the little blue box. Inside was a huge silver heart pendant on a black silk cord. Maddy stared at it for a second and then remembered. A few months ago, she and Brian had been window-shopping in Union Square. They had just gotten Starbucks, and Maddy had stopped in front of a display of jewelry in front of Tiffany. The heart pendant shone on a bed of gray velvet. "Ohmygod, look at that gorgeous thing," she'd said, tugging at Brian's sleeve. "That would look so perfect with my summer tops." She'd cast a sly, meaningful look at Brian.

"Dream on, babe," he'd said with a laugh. "Sunny

just got that same heart. It's like fifteen hundred dollars."

She had forgotten about it almost immediately, but Brian hadn't, obviously. Now here it was, right in front of her and she honestly couldn't have cared less. It looked different to her now, splashy and sort of cheap, for some reason. Maddy looked from the box to Brian's face. He was grinning, anticipating her reaction. So she did the only thing she could—she faked it.

"It's gorgeous!" she said. "I can't believe you remembered!" *It really is thoughtful,* she told herself.

"I can't believe I did either. It's like a miracle or something."

"Here, put it on me." She handed him the box. He lifted out the pendant and placed the cord around her throat, struggling a minute with the tiny catch at the back. Maddy stood and looked in the mirror. The heart shone on her tanned chest, but something about the modern, sleek design looked out of place with her white dress and the simple room around her.

Brian came up behind her and put his arms around her waist, watching their reflections in the mirror. "It looks awesome on you," he said. He kissed the side of her neck and then slid his hand up from her waist. Maddy giggled nervously.

"Come on—we're in my parents' room!"

"So?" He tried to kiss her again.

"Go away. I have to primp some more. Go talk to my Dad or something."

Brian rolled his eyes and reluctantly headed toward the door. Maddy could hear his footsteps slowly descending the stairs. She turned back to the mirror and covered the heart up with her hand. Outfit perfect. She removed her hand. Outfit weird. Maddy massaged her forehead, where a headache was starting to squeeze her temples, and followed her boyfriend down the stairs.

"Happy birthday, honey!" her mom sang out as she entered the kitchen. "You look beautiful. I can't believe I have a daughter who's turning seventeen!" She put her arms around Maddy and gave her a long hug.

"Thanks, Mom. I can't believe I'm seventeen either— kind of amazing." Maddy looked around the kitchen. A stack of plates was sitting on the table, along with a few bottles of wine, but there were no signs of cooking. "Where's all the food?"

"Oh, I'm not sure," her mother said airily, busying herself with a vase of flowers.

"What do you mean, you're not sure?" Maddy asked, confused.

"Just that—I don't really know where the food is. Maybe the raccoons ran off with it."

"Ha-ha. Something's up, Mom. You're terrible at keeping secrets."

Her mom picked up the vase. "You're right, honey. I'll tell you—we've decided to take you out to McDonald's for your birthday." The screen door banged behind her.

Maddy followed her onto the porch. "Very funny."

Her mother set the flowers on a little table. Maddy leaned against her side and laid her head on her mother's shoulder. Standing hand in hand, they were silent for a moment, listening to the peepers. Until Maddy realized something. "Um, Mom, where's Brian?"

"He's in the living room with Dad. They're having a nice chat." Maddy doubted that somehow. She'd better go rescue, well, both of them.

The soft, familiar colors of the living room glowed in the orange light of the lamps. Maddy paused quietly in the doorway. Neither her father nor Brian noticed her standing there. Darkness pressed at the windows, and the wooden coffee table was piled with books and copies of *Practical Winery & Vineyard*. Her dad was sitting in the big armchair, his legs crossed, one hand swirling wine in a glass. Even from the doorway, Maddy could see that he was gripping the glass more tightly than necessary. Brian sat in a studiously casual pose on the green velour sofa, arm flung over the back, ankle crossed over knee. He tapped a little on the sofa arm and whistled under his breath. Her dad looked strained.

"Ah, so . . . how do you like the vineyard, Brian?" he asked politely.

"It's really nice." There was another silence. "Really cool."

"Yes, well, we can't expect much the first year, of course, but after this fall we're going to double our vine capacity," Maddy's father said with more vigor. Brian's gaze started to wander. Her dad trailed off. The silence descended again. Her dad started to fiddle with the edge of a newspaper at his elbow.

"So, Maddy tells me you're going down to L.A. after this weekend?"

"Yeah, my buddies and I are staying with some people in Malibu."

"Oh, I see." Silence again.

Maddy thought that if she had to listen to Brian and her father make any more small talk, she was going to pull her hair out by the roots. Why did he always clam up like that around her parents? Sure, they were a little odd sometimes, but they were just parents, she thought. He acted so stupid and stiff around them. "Hey, guys," she said brightly, entering the room. Both of them turned toward her with obvious relief.

"Hi, honey!" Her dad practically leaped to his feet. "How's the birthday girl?"

"Great."

"Come on, you all, it's time for the birthday girl's dinner," her mother said, sticking her head in the room.

"Are you coming?" Maddy asked Brian, who was still sitting down.

"Yeah." He took his time getting off the sofa. Maddy followed her mom into the kitchen and stopped short just inside the door.

"Mom!" she cried. "I can't believe you brought the crown!" Sitting on the scrubbed round kitchen table was an object that resembled a Burger King crown with schizophrenia. It actually *was* an old Burger King crown—practically museum-quality. Dried macaroni, old pieces of faded yarn, shells, and plastic beads were stuck all over the gold cardboard with a liberal, crumbling layer of Elmer's glue. Maddy had made the crown at her own princess-themed sixth birthday party. Everyone had had a glorious, sticky, messy time decorating their own crowns. On the front, Maddy had written MADDY BIRTH-DAY GIRL in careful, wobbly print. She remembered being so proud that she'd made the *G* facing the right direction.

The crown had been preserved and trotted out every year until Maddy finally forbade its appearance at her twelfth-birthday pool party. Her mother had seemed to understand at the time, and the crown hadn't reappeared since—until now.

Maddy looked at her mom and dad. They were grinning. Brian stood in the doorway, looking confused. "You know, guys," she said, "at first I thought that, since

I'm seventeen, a tiara from Cartier would be nice, but after seeing this crown again, I've totally changed my mind." Her parents applauded as she placed it on her head and bowed, trying to keep the crown from crashing to the floor.

"Here, honey, get in a picture with Dad." Maddy's mother was wielding the digital camera. Obligingly, Maddy and her dad draped their arms around each other's shoulders and smiled. Then her father took the camera and everyone shuffled around.

"Now one with your mom." *Click.*

"Okay, now me and Brian," Maddy said. He was still standing forlornly in the doorway. "Come here, cutie." He came over. She put her arms around him and gave him a hug. "Are you having a good time?" she whispered.

He looked down at her. "Yeah, of course," he said, as if there were no other possible option.

"Okay, kids, smile!" Maddy's dad aimed the camera at them. *Click.*

"Let me see, Dad," Maddy took the camera and everyone bent over the tiny screen. She paged through a series of photos of the grapevines and the house before coming to the ones they had just taken. There were general murmurs of "Cute!" and "Good one" at the pictures of Maddy with her parents, but when she came to the one of Brian and her, everyone squinted at the screen.

Maddy could see why—it wasn't very good: Brian had his eyes closed for one thing, but it wasn't just that. His clothes looked too harsh and dark against the soft wood of the background and her white cotton dress, and they were standing kind of stiffly, their arms around each other's waists. It looked like they'd just met and had been told to stand still to have their photo taken.

"Well!" her mother said, turning away. "Very nice." Maddy could tell by the tone of her voice that her mom had noticed the dissonance also. Maddy tried to quell the tiny worm of worry inside her. Things were a little off, but they'd been apart for a while. Right now she and Brian were together—that was what mattered.

Chapter Twenty

✦

Where are we going, Mom?" Maddy asked. "I'm starving." She was starting to get a little annoyed. It was already nine thirty, and for the last ten minutes, she, Brian, and her parents had been weaving their way through the grapevines, up and down different rows, as if they were hunting something. Maddy's full skirt brushed her ankles as she walked. The full moon cast a ghostly white light over the field, and an abundance of stars were flung across the inky black sky.

Was this some sort of pre-dinner scavenger hunt her parents had cooked up? She could hear Brian's footsteps behind her. Up ahead, the adults reached the end of a row and turned right, disappearing.

"Oh, here you are! We were lost. I forgot where

you . . ." The rest of her mother's words were lost in an indistinct mumble.

What the hell was going on? Maddy walked faster and finally broke into a trot. She turned down the row her parents were in and skidded to a halt so fast that Brian, close behind her, almost sent her sprawling into the dirt.

There, in the middle of the grapevines, was the most beautiful feast she had ever seen, spread on a simple white cloth. Bunches of lavender, grasses, and daisies stood in big pottery pitchers down the center of the long table. Candles in clear glass holders were scattered between the flowers, spreading a warm yellow glow over everything.

Vineyard tomatoes and thick white slices of fresh mozzarella with basil stood at one end. A bowl heaped with arugula, endive, and radicchio was liberally sprinkled with—Maddy laughed—blue cheese crumbles. Crowded near the salad was a platter of cold salmon with dill, drizzled with a silky cream sauce. A gorgeous chocolate torte stood next to a white bowl of glowing raspberry sauce. David stood next to Fred, leaning his palms on the end of the table. Maddy's eyes met his, and he grinned. "The torte is coffee-chocolate," he said.

"Wow!" Maddy exclaimed. "This is so gorgeous! Look at all of this!" Everyone was grinning. "Whose idea was this?" She looked questioningly at her mother. Mom was smiling and shaking her head.

"It wasn't me, honey."

Maddy looked around. "It wasn't you?" David's grin broadened as he saw the realization dawn on her face. Maddy looked at him, amazed. "*You*? I can't believe you'd—" She caught herself and quickly tore her eyes away from his.

He looked down and brushed an invisible crumb from the table. "It's nothing—just some stuff I put together this afternoon." His voice was low, but the pleasure in it was unmistakable.

"Arrmmhh." Brian cleared his throat.

"Oh, I'm sorry. David, this is Brian, my . . . boyfriend." She wondered if the tiny pause had been apparent to anyone else. The two boys eyed each other—one very tall and lean, clean-shaven, with curly light brown hair, the other dark-haired and blue-eyed, a three-day scruff on his chin.

David jerked his head once. "Hey."

"Hey." Brian stuck his hands in his pockets. David reached out and plucked a piece of yarn off Maddy's shoulder. He held it out. "This fell off your crown," he said solemnly.

"Oh! Thanks." She took the yarn. "It sheds some-times."

"I noticed," he replied with a funny look on his face.

"Well, okay!" Maddy's father said heartily, looking from Brian's furrowed brow to David's bland expression with the air of a hockey referee trying to head off a brawl on the ice. "Let's eat."

The food was incredible. Maddy couldn't stop eating. Her mom insisted David tell her the recipe for the cream sauce, and he laughed and shook his head, saying that Mondavi chefs would hunt him down if he let that gem get out. Maddy looked around the table at everyone's faces, illuminated by the soft candlelight, the wind blowing up the rows and occasionally lifting one end of the tablecloth. This had to be one of her best birthdays yet.

"Well, honey, this is the first birthday here at the vineyard," Maddy's father said, glancing around the table and smiling.

"Stop, Dad, I can hear the violins starting," Maddy teased.

Suddenly, there was a thud next to her. Maddy looked over to find Brian lying on the ground, flat on his back, lying on top of the wooden chair he had been sitting on. A chair leg was lying in the dirt a few feet away.

"Oh my God, Brian. Are you okay?" She leaned down.

"What happened?" Maddy's mother asked with concern. Everyone was craning to look over at Brian, who had picked himself up and was now brushing the clingy dust from his blue shirt, his face red.

"I was just sitting there and the chair bottom busted through." He picked up the chair. The woven rush seat

had a giant ragged hole in it. "And a leg snapped off."
He sounded like he was mad but trying not to show it.

Maddy's eyes widened, and involuntarily, she locked
eyes with David across the table. She could tell he was
thinking the same thing she was—the only difference
was, he looked like he was about to start laughing hyster-
ically. Brian caught the look and his eyes narrowed.
"What's going on?" he asked slowly.

Maddy glared at David, whose face had started to
turn purple from holding in his laughter. "Nothing, I'm
sorry. It's just, one of the chairs in the shed was a
casualty of a minor paint fight we might have had. We
put it aside to take it up to the repair shed, but—"

"Dad must have gotten it when we were getting chairs
for dinner, not realizing it was broken," David finished.
Fred nodded, looking a little sheepish.

"I grabbed one that was sitting right by the door," he
said.

"Oh, well, let's just get that bucket over there,"
Maddy's mom jumped in. "We can turn it upside down
and—"

"I'll sit on it," David interrupted. "Brian, take my
seat." Brian looked suspicious for a minute and then
moved toward the foot of the table. David vacated his
seat and settled down on the upturned metal bucket
across from the birthday girl.

"Thanks."

David shrugged. "Sure."

Fred leaned over to Maddy's mother. "Debbie, I wanted to tell you that I did some pricing on a new mower—they're really exorbitant."

"I completely forgot, Fred, I talked to a guy from the seed place and he has a mower he might be selling," her father said.

David rolled his eyes at Maddy. "Business again?"

She smiled. "Why are they so boring?"

Then, with an innocent air, David said, "I wonder if that's how we sounded at the furniture store?"

"*David,*" Maddy kicked him under the table. He widened his eyes and gave her a "Who, me?" look. Brian looked up from his fish.

"What happened at the furniture store?" he asked Maddy.

"Nothing," she said.

"Something happened. Unless you're into reminiscing about sofa-shopping now," Brian insisted.

Maddy sighed and aimed another invisible kick at David's shin. "It was just a funny misunderstanding, that's all. We were picking out furniture for the tasting room, David and I, and the salesman called David my *husband,*" she explained, stifling a giggle. She looked over at Brian with an expectant smile, waiting for him to laugh at the absurdity of the situation, but his face was stony.

She hurried ahead. "So, we were just joking around

and David said, 'Oh, yeah, we hardly have any furniture,' and the guy asked if we were newlyweds and I had to explain that I was keeping my maiden name and it was all just totally ridiculous." David's laughter erupted like he'd been holding his breath until now. His laugh was infectious and Maddy giggled also, remembering how earnest the salesman had been. She couldn't help it. But Brian just sat there silently, his eyebrows knit together.

Suddenly, Maddy's gaze locked onto David's across the table. He smiled right into her eyes, his face open and engaging. Before Maddy could stop herself, she smiled right back at him, despite Brian sitting right next to her. Her heart started beating faster and her palms felt clammy. What was going on? Why was she having this kind of reaction? *You know why,* a little voice in her head piped up. *You've known for a while now. Be quiet!* she insisted. *Oh, just face it,* the voice went on. *You want David.* Oh. My. God. *No!* She glanced at Brian as if he could read her mind. But she didn't need to worry—he wasn't even looking at her. He was staring off into space, gazing over the tops of the vines.

Maddy stared down at her lap, trying to calm her racing thoughts. Her *boyfriend* was sitting two feet away. *This is David,* she reminded herself. *David. Remember? Work buddy?* Platonic *friend? Don't panic,* she told herself. *Stay calm. Brian is your boyfriend. Just focus on him and everything will be fine.*

Chapter Twenty-one

✦

On Sunday night, Maddy wandered out to the orchard after Brian was ensconced safely in his car, probably doing ninety down the highway on his way back to San Francisco. Her parents had gone into town for groceries and ice cream, but Maddy had begged off, saying she needed to decompress a little. And she did. Her nerves had been rubbed raw by the tension of the weekend. Between Brian, David, and her confusion, she had felt like she was being pulled tight enough to pluck like a guitar string. She needed some time just to think and sort out her mass of tangled emotions.

Maddy took a deep breath, gazing at the hills colored red, gold, and pink. She could feel some of the stress slipping away with the setting sun. The vineyard looked beautiful with the flowers in full bloom and light on the trees. But despite all of it, she knew the weekend hadn't gone right at all—not like she'd expected. Brian had been so distant. And then there'd been the craziness of her birthday dinner . . . and David. There was definitely a connection between them, but she *had* to make sure it didn't go further. She had to figure out Brian's deal before she could even think about David.

"Hey," David's familiar voice said softly. Maddy spun around; she hadn't heard him approach. "I was going to get my iPod out of the shed. . . ."

His curly hair was still wet from a shower. His skin glowed from the water and the fading sunlight. Maddy nodded. Without saying anything else, he fell in beside her. They strolled silently around the edges of the orchard, David occasionally reaching out to slap a tree trunk under the deep, spreading branches. The setting sun pierced the leaves, painting their faces as they passed beneath. It could have been sort of awkward, walking like this, but Maddy felt comforted by David's presence.

"So, are you okay?" David finally asked. Maddy was quiet for a long moment. David shook his head. "Sorry. It's none of my business."

"No, it's okay. I'm just so confused. This weekend didn't turn out anything like I thought."

He looked at her. "How come?"

They had almost reached the end of the orchard. In front of them, the grapevines stretched in curving rows. She hesitated. "Brian." She felt a little weird saying this, but she really just needed to talk to someone. "It just seemed so different with us this time than it usually is."

"Usually? You mean like down in the city?"

"Yeah. He just seemed awkward out here. We were kind of having trouble finding things to talk about."

David nodded. "That's hard."

"I know," Maddy went on. "I don't even know if we're still meant to be together." She stole a glance sideways at David. He had stopped walking and was gazing out over the hills, his hands in his pockets. His face was serious.

"That must be rough. But, you know, I don't think he's good enough for someone like you." He turned toward her and put his hands on her shoulders. Maddy inhaled sharply. He was looking into her eyes, his gaze direct and clear. Gently, he slid one hand under her hair at the back of her neck and drew her a little closer. Maddy's heart was pounding. "I wasn't impressed by him," he said softly. His face was so near that his breath tickled her cheek. "He just seems like a rich jerk." He leaned down. Maddy pulled back abruptly. For an instant, they stared at each other, eyes wide.

"What are you doing?" she asked.

"I . . ." He looked totally taken aback.

"Are you coming on to me? Because in case you hadn't noticed, I have a boyfriend." At the back of her mind, she knew she was being unfair. They both felt a connection, but she couldn't stop herself. All of her confused, frustrated feelings poured out of her. "I'm not just up for grabs."

"But you just said it wasn't working out," he reminded her.

"All I said was that I was *thinking* about things! I didn't say we were breaking up or anything."

"Well, you could've fooled me." David took a step backward and narrowed his eyes. "You really want to be with that guy?" His voice was scornful.

"You don't even know him!" Maddy shot back. "And the last thing I need right now is you jumping all over me! Thanks a lot—I guess that's what I get for confiding in you."

"Fine. Then I guess I was wrong about Brian being too good for you. I take it back—it looks like you two are perfect for each other."

"Maybe we are!" Maddy shouted at him. "He should be perfect for a *spoiled suburban brat* like me!" She emphasized the last words and watched his face harden.

"That was a long time ago. And I already apologized," David said through clenched teeth.

"Yeah, well, maybe you should say it again." She crossed her arms over her chest defiantly.

"Why? I was right all along—any girl who likes that narcissistic asshole can't be anything but a spoiled brat."

Maddy stared at him, her hands clenching into fists, nails digging painfully into her palms. She turned and ran back toward the house, her heart pounding in her ears. As she fled, she shot a quick glance over her shoulder. David stood alone among the trees, watching her, with the setting sun at his back.

✦ ✦ ✦

Maddy was sitting on her bed, runny-nosed and blotchy-faced, thinking dully that she should get up and find a tissue, when someone knocked on the door. "C-come in," she sniffled, giving up on the tissue and wiping her nose on her arm.

Maddy's mom opened the door and took one look at her daughter's swollen eyelids and matted hair. "I saw you running up to the house," she said, sitting next to Maddy on the bed and putting her arms around her. "You looked pretty upset." Maddy gave up all semblance of control and started sobbing again, resting her face against her mother's shoulder.

After a few minutes, her sobs began to taper off. Her

mom handed her a tissue. "What is it, sweetie? I know this has been a hard week for you."

"It has. I don't know what to do!" Maddy wailed all of a sudden. Her mother looked concerned.

"About what?"

Maddy paused and took a deep breath. She wasn't sure how to articulate what she was feeling. "It's just that I feel so confused. I don't know what I want. It was so weird when Brian was here—he didn't even seem like the same person I remembered. Like, he wasn't even listening when I was talking. He was never like that at home."

Her mom's eyebrows knitted. "I noticed that things seemed a little awkward between the two of you."

"So awkward! He's changed and I don't know why."

Maddy's mother considered this for a moment. "Here's a thought," she said. "Did you ever think that maybe it's not Brian who's changed, but *you*?"

She shook her head. "No, I don't think that's it—I mean, it's only been a couple of months."

"But think about it, Maddy. Brian's been in the city this whole time, just like before. You've been the one in the new environment."

Maddy was quiet. She hadn't thought about it like that before. Her mom went on. "You know, honey, I haven't mentioned this to you before, because you did seem to like Brian a lot and he's not a *bad* person, but I have never really thought that he was smart enough or kind enough for you."

Maddy started to protest but something stopped her. Wasn't that sort of what David had said? "Oh, Mom," she said. "You're just a little biased, don't you think?"

Her mother stood up from the bed. "Not really. Now, what are you going to do?"

"I don't know yet," Maddy said thoughtfully.

"Whatever you do decide," her mother said, giving Maddy a pat on the arm, "be strong."

"I will, Mom."

"I'd expect nothing less from my own daughter."

Maddie paused. "Mom, I–I'm sorry. For everything, all of it. For what a brat I've been all summer. It was incredibly dumb and disrespectful to throw that party. And I didn't mean what I said about the vineyard being stupid. I was just frustrated."

"Well, it's all in the past. I'm just so glad we've had this time together up here, as a family, this summer," her mother said. "I don't think it's turned out the way any of us expected." She reached over and gave Maddy a little squeeze before softly closing the door behind her.

✦ ✦ ✦

Maddy continued lying on her bed for a while after her mother left, staring out the window at the night sky. She knew what she had to do. Her stomach did a little flip as she thought about calling Brian, but her instincts told her it was the right decision. She looked at the bedside clock. Nine thirty. *Be strong,* she told herself, and dialed him on her cell.

He answered right away. "Hey, what's up?"

"Nothing—how's it going?" she said automatically, hugging a pillow to her chest.

"Okay. Just hanging out by the pool with Chad and the guys." Great—there were people there.

"Well, um, do you think you could go inside or somewhere private? I have to talk to you about something important."

"Can't it wait until later? We're just starting a hand of poker."

"No, Brian, it can't. Please go inside." She was surprised at how calm her voice was.

He sighed. She could hear the scraping of a chair. "Be right back, guys," he said away from the phone. There was a long pause. "Okay, I'm in the living room. What's so important?"

She took a deep breath. "Brian, I don't know if this is working anymore." She waited for a second. Silence on the other end. "I just think we might be growing apart."

More silence. And then, "Are you breaking up with me?" He sounded incredulous.

"No! I mean . . . maybe. I don't know." She could hear him breathing.

"What's going on with you? You're acting like a totally different person."

"I–" The words were on her lips to deny it but she checked herself. "I know." More silence. She got the impression that wasn't the response he was expecting. A voice in the background yelled, "Come on, Kilburn!"

"Do you have to go?" Maddy asked, since he still wasn't saying anything.

"Yeah."

She waited, but after a minute, she realized that there wasn't going to be any more. She didn't know if he was mad or surprised or sad. Apparently, he wasn't going to tell her. "Okay. Maybe I'll see you–"

Click.

He hung up. Maddy stared at the phone in shock. Then she put it down on the bed and shrugged to herself. She guessed she had her answer to what he was feeling, and it was neither surprise nor sadness.

She rolled over and switched off the light. The soft darkness surrounded her. She tried to evaluate her feelings. Why wasn't she more upset? Brian had been her boyfriend for over a year. She felt kind of weird that she wasn't devastated. Then it dawned on her. She had already gone through all the sadness that comes with breaking up—only for her, it had come before, not after. The phone conversation with Brian had made it official, but in her mind the deed had been done for days. And it felt right. Exhaustion overwhelmed her as she drew the sheet up under her chin. She listened to the porch cricket's nightly song and let slumber overtake her.

Chapter Twenty-two

✦

Bright sun streamed onto Maddy's face. She closed her eyes against the glare and rolled over, stuffing her head into the pillow. "Arrrgg," she groaned. Yesterday's drama had left her with a headache worse than a hangover. *Why* had she rejected David? She had really screwed up this time. *You totally blew your chance with an awesome guy,* her helpful inner voice informed her. *Nice work ruining what's left of your summer.*

"*Gah!*" she growled aloud and sat up. Furiously, she kicked back the sheet and climbed out of bed. Opening the doors to her porch, she leaned out over the railing. The Napa morning was glowing as always. The vines were silvery with dew, and the air was fresh and piney. These facts did nothing to lift Maddy's spirits. *"Ahhh!"* she shouted out into the yard, not worrying who heard.

Maddy slammed the balcony doors and turned back into her room. Man, it was a mess. She hooked yesterday's dirty clothes out from under the bed, dumped them into the hamper, and pulled on cutoffs and a green T-shirt, jerking the dresser drawers so hard one of them cracked. She took a deep breath and forced herself to unclench her aching jaw. Her headache continued drilling farther into her temples. She closed her eyes. A vision of herself screaming at David in the orchard and his shocked, angry expression flashed through her mind.

Maddy pounded down the stairs to the kitchen, where she gulped an enormous glass of water and pressed a damp paper towel to her forehead for a minute to try to cool off her raging thoughts. The room was empty. She wondered where everyone was and then looked at the clock for the first time. It was only six. Mom and Dad weren't even awake yet. Whatever. She definitely wasn't going back to bed.

She yanked open the back door and crossed the yard to the shed where they kept the gardening tools. The threat of a nice collection of snakes, mice, and lizards in the dark, musty depths always terrified her, but today she didn't even pause to look around. She grabbed a trowel, basket, and rake and stomped outside to the garden. She had to do *something* today, and it wasn't going to be in the tasting room. She couldn't just lie around or she'd wind up jumping out a window. She might as well garden. A pang of sadness pierced her frustration as she thought of David, alone in the tasting room. Today he was going to install shelving to hold the wine bottles. She really wanted to see how it looked. But more than that, she wanted to see *him*. Maddy shook her head. *Fat chance*, she told herself. *You can bet that he certainly never wants to see you again. Why humiliate yourself even more, Madeline?*

Rows of peppers, eggplant, zucchini, and tomatoes stood neatly, soaking up the morning sun, which was already strong, even this early in the morning. The carrots and onions were almost choked with weeds. Maddy put her tools down and started with a row of carrots. On her knees in the sandy yellow soil, the sun beating through her thin T-shirt, she yanked out one weed for losing her temper in the orchard. Another was for wasting half the summer worrying about Brian. A giant prickly nettle was for not seeing how great David was right from the beginning. The cluster of dandelions was for all the chances to kiss him she'd never get, and the huge, spiny thing was for her parents dragging her up to Napa so she could get all confused, instead of letting her enjoy her old life back in the city.

Maddy sat back on her heels for a minute and wiped at the sweat on her dusty forehead with the back of her hand. She took a breath and looked behind her at the trail of yanked-up weeds left in her wake. She felt a little better.

"Wow, this is great." Maddy looked up. Her mom stood at the edge of the garden in her old blue bathrobe, holding a glass of iced tea. She handed the glass to her grubby daughter. "I thought you could use this. Dad and I were watching you out the window." Maddy got to her feet, accepted the frosty, wet glass, and downed the tea in three long gulps. "You know, it's nice to see you enjoying your work here in the vineyard. You've adjusted so well since the beginning of the summer."

Maddy smiled grimly. If "adjusted well" meant she was confused and mad about everything in her life, then her mom was right—she was doing just peachy. "Yeah, well, I needed a little exercise this morning," Maddy explained.

Her mother smiled and turned to go back to the house. Halfway across the yard, she stopped. "Oh, Maddy, I almost forgot. David and Fred are coming for lunch today."

"What? I thought they only came to dinner!" Maddy cried. Her mom looked at her strangely. Maddy dropped her eyes and started gathering some of the weeds up into a little pile.

"Daddy and Fred are going into town for the Winemakers License Hearing at the town council, and you know that's a big deal. So I thought they should come straight here after, and we'll all have a nice sit-down lunch together, to celebrate clearing another hurdle."

Maddy sank back on her heels. Great. She'd get to stare David in the face for an entire meal. Her headache started coming back. Then her eyes widened as something stirred in her mind. David had accused her of being the girl he'd always thought she was, the spoiled brat from the city. But what if she could show him that she wasn't—that she had changed? What if she could catch him by surprise?

Maddy leaped to her feet. "Hey, Mom," she called across the yard. "You know, I could make lunch today, if you want." Her mother stopped short and turned around slowly, an incredulous look on her face.

"You want to cook?" she asked carefully.

"Yeah, sure. I'd love to."

"Well," Maddy's mom said delicately, "that would be great. What do you want to make?"

She hadn't gotten that far yet. Maddy looked around the garden. "Um, I'll do something with the veggies here."

Her mother looked doubtful. "Okay, well, that's fine. Can you have it ready by one?"

"Sure!" Maddy sounded a lot more confident than she felt. She looked around the garden as her mother disappeared back into the house. The vegetables stood shining in the sun, looking intimidatingly raw. She groaned a little to herself. What had come over her? Was it momentary insanity? She had made scrambled eggs and spaghetti before but . . . eggplant? Maddy rose and walked over to the shiny purple vegetables. She picked one and held it up. It was light. The smooth skin and springy flesh underneath made it feel disturbingly alive—like it might actually be an animal and not a plant. Maddy turned it slowly in her hand. *How the heck do you cook this? Do you eat the skin? What about the hard green leaves on top?* What the hell? Everyone was always raving about how good eggplant was. She'd figure it out. She picked six big ones and set them aside.

Picking the zucchini, Maddy found that they were covered with spiky little hairs, which she'd never seen before, and the tomatoes were all misshapen and bulgy, not round like she was used to. There was something else growing that she couldn't even identify—it was a green object with a long, feathery top and a bulbous bottom. It kind of looked like deformed celery. Whatever it was, there was a lot of it, so Maddy picked several of those too, along with onions and peppers. At least those looked normal.

She loaded everything into a basket and lugged it across the lawn, feeling the sun beating down on the back of her neck, and banged back into the kitchen. Her parents sat at the table, the newspaper spread out in front of them, sipping their coffee. Her father was peacefully munching a plate of toast. In the corner, the radio was playing classical music.

Maddy dropped the basket on the floor and scowled at them, panting. The dirt from the garden had mixed with the sweat on her arms, leaving long dirty streaks. Her head was pounding and the mosquito bites on the backs of her knees itched ferociously.

"Mom says you're cooking for us, sweetie!" Her father chirped.

"Mmmm." Maddy stomped over to the fridge and took out some blueberry pie, which she began devouring straight out of the pan without cutting a piece. She realized her parents had put down the newspaper and were staring at her.

"Pie for breakfast, Maddy?" her mother inquired. "Do you want me to make you some eggs?"

"No!" she snapped, and then controlled herself. "I mean, I'm fine, thanks, Mom."

"All right." Her mother wandered over to the basket of vegetables and sank down on her heels to peer in. "You picked some fennel! That'll be interesting."

"Fennel?" That must be that weird bulbous celery thing with the feathery top. "Oh, yeah. That's what I thought too."

Her mom rose and gave her an absent smile. "Well, have fun. Daddy has his hearing soon, and I promised the North Napa Vineyard Association I'd staff a booth at the outreach fair this morning. But everyone will be back by one."

"Great!" Maddy sounded far more enthusiastic than she felt. "See you then. I have everything under control."

Chapter Twenty-three

✦

Maddy stood at the kitchen counter, holding a giant chopping knife and eyeing the stack of vegetables heaped in front of her. Somehow, these were going to turn into lunch for five, though she had no idea how that was going to happen.

It was sweltering in the kitchen, despite the open windows. The thought of turning on the stove wasn't very appealing, but Maddy had the feeling people wouldn't be impressed by raw onions and peppers. She had tied her hair into a bun and put on a loose cotton tank top, but it didn't make much difference. It was just hot. There was no way around it. The sweat beaded up on her arms and at the edges of her hairline. A trickle ran from her neck down the front of her chest. Bleah.

All she wanted to do was leave this inferno of a room, pour herself a glass of iced tea, and lie on the porch chair with a fan aimed directly at her face.

But she couldn't, so instead she poised her knife as she had seen David do, and brought it down on one of the eggplants with a resounding whack. The vegetable split into two pale halves, which lay in front of her on the cutting board, rocking slightly. Maddy leaned forward to examine them. All sorts of little seeds were suspended in some sort of spongy, stringy stuff in the middle. What did you do with those? Could you eat them? She shrugged and chopped four others into halves and the halves into pieces. That should do it. It looked like kind of a lot, but there were five people eating.

The fennel was even more daunting. *Eat the tops? Cut the tops off? Eat the thing raw? Cook it?* Finally, she just sliced the whole thing up, feathery tops and all. The tomatoes were easy, although two had worms in them, which was *revolting*. She accidentally dropped some pieces on the floor and then stepped on them, which created tomato slime all over the place that she had to stop and mop up.

The peppers were the nicest looking—dark green, slender, and shiny. The onions, though, made her eyes tear. While she was blundering to the sink to splash water on her face, she knocked the entire cutting board, heaped with sliced vegetables, onto the floor. Damn it! She forgot her stinging eyes and knelt quickly to gather up the scattered pieces. What David didn't know wouldn't hurt him. She picked the biggest pieces of dust off the pile and then put the spill out of her mind. It was already twelve thirty. How the hell had that happened? The only lunch in sight was a battered pile of raw vegetables. She flashed on the image of David standing at this very counter, his knife flashing like magic, transforming a pile of olives into tiny bits, chatting effortlessly the entire time. *Well, you're a beginner, Maddy, but you can do it. Just think of his face when he realizes you cooked this whole lunch.*

She wiped her arm across her forehead, grabbed a large pot out of the cabinet, dumped every last piece in, and then turned the burner on. There. Now, what went with cooked vegetables? Well, she knew how to make pasta. And they could spoon the vegetables over the top. Maddy searched through the pantry but couldn't find any of the familiar blue-and-red boxes. She shut the door and stood tapping her fingers on her cheek, thinking. They'd had pasta just the other night. Maddy remembered seeing a pile of it on the counter. In a flash of inspiration, she opened the refrigerator door. There it was—a plastic bag of noodles sitting right in the front. She grabbed it, filled another pot with water and set it on a high flame.

The smell of smoke distracted her from the pasta

water. Damn! She peered into the vegetable pot. Some of the veggies were burning and stuck to the bottom of the pot, but other pieces still looked alarmingly raw. Maddy grabbed a long wooden spoon and poked at the mess. Maybe she should take it off the burner and switch to the microwave or something. Before she could do that, she was interrupted by a splashing, sizzling sound. The pasta water was ready—boiling over, in fact. She turned down the flame and dumped in the noodles. They looked strange—soft instead of stiff. But, it was twelve forty-five, and she still had to set the table. She thought again of the long table set among the cool green leaves of the field. Well, she wasn't doing that. The table out on the lawn would be fine. The kitchen was like a circle of hell right now. There was no way they could eat inside. Maddy pulled a stack of plates down from the shelves and added silverware. Paper napkins would have to suffice—it was just lunch. If anyone (*David*) didn't think that was classy enough, tough. Except there weren't any napkins—at least, none that she could find, and she didn't know where her mother kept the cloth ones. She grabbed a roll of paper towels. Why had she ever thought that this little enterprise would *improve* her foul mood?

She banged out the back door and across the lawn. It wasn't much cooler outside, and the picnic table at the rear of the lawn was baking in the sun. Maddy didn't really have time to think about it, though. She hurriedly dealt out place settings for five and dashed back across the lawn.

The kitchen smelled ominously of burning, and smoke was beginning to wisp from the vegetable pot. *Crap!* Maddy realized she'd forgotten to take it off the burner. She quickly set the vegetables aside on the counter and peered anxiously into the pot of noodles. Something wasn't right. Instead of the nicely al dente strands she expected, the surface was covered with broken-up pieces of noodle, and the water was all cloudy. She looked at the clock—she hadn't screwed up this time. It had only been eight minutes since she put the pasta in the water. So why did it look so weird? She stabbed a fork at the mess, but only succeeded in breaking up the depressingly mushy noodles into even smaller pieces. It looked years overdone. Lovely. Just lovely.

Maddy stood staring at the pot, breathing in the smoke that hung in a little cloud around the kitchen ceiling until she heard her mother's voice on the porch. "Need any help?" She turned around. Her mom was peering through the screen door.

"No!" Maddy leaped at the door. "Go sit down outside. I'm almost ready. . . ."

"Oh, good. Dad and Fred are back and they're starving." Her mother trailed off. Maddy turned her attention back to the more urgent tasks at hand. She gingerly tried to pick the noodle pieces out of the water with two big salad forks and managed to transfer most of them to a bowl, though they were dangerously fragile. The vegetables looked completely bizarre. For the most part, they were an indistinguishable, blackened stew, but for some reason, the onion stood out in big, raw-looking pieces. Maddy scraped it all on top of the noodles and, in a pitiful attempt to make the dish attractive, picked a sprig of Mom's fresh basil from the pot on the windowsill and stuck it in the middle, where it looked garishly green in contrast.

Maddy picked up the giant bowl and a serving spoon and headed toward the door. Damn. *Drinks*. She set the bowl down and opened the fridge. The tea pitcher was about an inch full. The entire family had drunk it by the gallon all summer and Mom had picked today not to make any? Maddy looked around wildly and spied a packet of Crystal Light sitting on the counter. Mixed-berry flavor. Fine. She filled a pitcher and dumped in the powder. It turned the water a thoroughly unnatural red. Maddy loaded the whole business onto a tray. This is the lunch she was going to win David back with? One bowl of mush and red-40-laden water. She gritted her teeth and pushed through the screen door toward the table on the lawn.

Chapter Twenty-four

◆

Everyone was already sitting around the table. Maddy tried not to notice David's figure at one end. The lawn seemed very long as she bore her tray in front of her like some ridiculous offering. She looked like hell, too—dirty, smelly, and unshowered. The thought occurred to her that she matched the food—*totally unappealing*.

She looked everywhere but at David as she set the tray down on the table.

"What's this dish called, Maddy?" Fred asked. He looked very different in his neatly pressed slacks and sport shirt. She'd never seen him in anything but jeans.

"Ah . . . Eggplant Surprise." She sank down into a chair and sneaked a hopeful glance at David. He was staring at the empty water glass in front of him, a studiedly casual expression pasted on his face. Maddy turned her gaze to the table. It looked dismal. The sun was beating down on everything in sight. Her father had almost sweated through his shirt. Maddy's mind flashed on the image of her birthday dinner, the gracefully set table, the platters of luscious dishes, the glasses and china glittering in the flickering candlelight—and David's proud, smiling face. She almost had to shut her eyes against the scene in front her. Before her sat a hurriedly set table in the harsh glare of the noon sun, complete with one roll of paper towels and a lonely bowl of vegetables.

Fred lifted the pitcher of red liquid. "Can I pour anyone some . . . Kool-Aid?" He paused quizzically on the last word.

"Crystal Light," Maddy muttered. Fred looked at the pitcher more closely.

"Right! Crystal Light, anyone?"

"Sure." Her dad gamely held out his glass.

Maddy could barely keep from dropping her eyes as her mother's spoon dipped into the serving bowl. The heat from the vegetables had continued cooking the pasta even more, which was unfortunate—it looked even more like mush than it had in the kitchen. Plus, now that some of it was ladled out, she could see that she had grossly overestimated how much five people could eat. The huge mound of the stuff in the bowl was easily enough for twenty. Her father looked at his plate as if something on it was about to jump up and bite him, but he quickly recovered. Maddy watched in anguish as David's plate was filled.

Everyone at the table gradually fell silent as the food was handed around. David was the last to get his portion. Maddy could hardly look at him, but he accepted his plate of the frightening substance readily and then, to her surprise, looked directly at her. He shot her a disarming smile. Maddy's pulse shot into the stratosphere and she felt her face turn flaming red. Ohmygod. What did that mean? He didn't hate her? No, he was probably feeling sorry for her and her hideous attempt at cooking. *It's a look of pity,* Maddy told herself glumly.

"I think that David, as the Ironstone Vineyard resident chef, should try the dish first so he can give us his professional opinion," her father said brightly.

Lovely, Dad. Thank you very much, Maddy thought.

David obligingly raised his heaping fork and took a large bite. He chewed for a minute, frowning slightly. Maddy found herself holding her breath. She couldn't tear her eyes away from his face.

David erupted in a convulsion of coughing. Everyone started in alarm.

"David!" Maddy's mother exclaimed. "Are you all right?"

Instead of answering, David leaped up from his chair,

knocking it over, and raced toward the house, where he disappeared inside the kitchen. The group, sitting in stunned silence, could hear the faucet running in the kitchen and loud slurping sounds. After a long moment—approximately seven or eight years, in Maddy's estimation—David appeared on the porch again and walked slowly toward the table. He stopped when he reached them, his face a slightly more normal shade of pink.

"Okay?" Fred asked cautiously.

"It's good," David said in a strangled voice. He picked up his overturned chair, and sat down. Maddy couldn't resist. She reached for her own fork and ever so carefully placed a tiny bit of eggplant in her mouth. The effect was instantaneous—heat exploded down her throat, her lips and tongue turning numb almost immediately. It took all of her willpower not to repeat David's performance. She coughed violently and chugged twelve ounces of Crystal Light. She set her glass down with a shudder and looked around the table. Now everyone was staring at her.

Maddy's mother finally broke the silence. "You know," she said, poking at a piece of green pepper with her fork, "just out of curiosity, did I *happen* to mention that we're growing jalapeño peppers as well as sweet peppers in the garden?"

Maddy flopped back in her chair, her cheeks burning

now instead of her mouth. She recalled the beautiful little dark green peppers she had admired. She had chopped up nearly a dozen.

"I'm impressed, though, Mad, that you took a stab at the pasta. It's so delicate," her mom hurried on.

At the other end of the table, David spoke for the first time. Maddy jumped at the sound of his voice. "How long did you boil it for?"

"Eight minutes." She stared determinedly at the planks of the table.

Her father cleared his throat. "Well, that might be why it's a tad . . . soft. You're only meant to boil fresh pasta for a minute or two at the absolute most."

Fresh pasta? That explained why it was in the fridge.

Staring at her wrecked attempt at cooking, Maddy could feel the tears prickling behind her eyes. No. *No.* She would not start crying like a little kid in front of David because her lunch was not the perfect representation of New Maddy. *No.* But it was useless. She could feel red patches start to form on her face, like usual, and her throat swelled and ached. She blinked furiously and stared up at the sky.

"Mads." Her mom reached over to pat her arm. "It's okay." Maddy moved away.

"I'm fine," she said, hearing the thickness in her voice. The first tear dropped onto a piece of onion on her plate. *Stop it, you idiot,* she ordered herself furiously.

Another tear splattered onto her wadded-up paper towel. "Excuse me," she said, standing up abruptly. She had to get out of here or she was going to bawl in front of everyone. Her parents were looking at her with concern. Fred was politely gazing at a beetle wending its way across the planks of the table. And David stared right at her, his brows knit. Maddy turned and fled across the lawn to the house, her humiliation complete.

❖ ❖ ❖

Maddy stood in the spray of the outdoor shower at the side of the house. From her bedroom window, she had watched everyone trickle away after lunch—her parents and Fred to the vine fields and David (her heart sank) toward the cottage. It was just as well, she thought. She needed to be alone. The cool spray felt incredible after the hot, dusty morning she'd spent in the garden and the sweaty episode in the kitchen. Around her the redwood walls of the little enclosed cubicle were glistening wet. Maddy's feet stood on another platform of redwood. The sun poured through the open top, splashing shadows onto her body. She leaned back to let the water soak her hair and worked in a dollop of Kiehl's shampoo. She scrubbed herself all over with lemon-scented soap and let the water sluice it off.

Maddy sighed and shut off the shower. All she

wanted to do was go straight upstairs to her room and fall asleep for about three hours—no, make that three years. She patted at her hair and wrapped herself in a thick white towel. She opened the door. David was standing immediately outside.

Maddy jumped, banging her head on the doorjamb, and let out an idiotic little squeak, like a mouse that had been stepped on. "Ow!" she said, holding the side of her head.

He was holding a backpack in his hand. He looked as surprised as she did. "Hey," he said softly.

Maddy could hardly look at him. God, what did he think of her now? The awful lunch, and then running away *crying*? "Hi," she managed, staring at his tan toes.

"Um, I was looking for a bucket. I don't know what I did with the one that was in the tasting room, so—"

Maddy clutched her towel a little tighter. "I'm, um, sorry about, you know, earlier." He didn't say anything, just waited. "I mean, running off like that . . ." He looked at her. "I'm just . . . under a lot of pressure right now." Her voice cracked on the last few words, and she could feel the tears building up *again*.

He reached out for her, like he might try to give her a hug. Maddy stepped away slightly and stood there, feeling miserable and stupid, tasting the tears that were now running down her cheeks to her lips. His voice was urgent and quiet. "I don't know what you're thinking about, but I hope when you get it figured out . . . you'll tell me."

For a long minute, they both just stood there, staring at each other. Maddy wanted to just *say* it—everything that was on her mind, everything that had gone wrong and right all summer long. His eyes were so big and dark, she just wanted to lose herself in them. Finally, she whispered, "Yeah," and rushed past him, almost knocking him over. *Yet another graceful exit for Ms. Madeline Sinclaire.* She ran down the path, feeling like she was going to implode.

Later that afternoon, Maddy was kneeling in the bean rows, watching an orb-weaving spider spin a huge web on the garden fence while she piled pinto beans into a basket with both hands. A few feet away, the tomatoes hung plump and red. One looked ripe enough to fall off the vine. It looked scrumptious. Maddy sat back on her heels, plucked the tomato. and bit into it like an apple. The juice ran down her chin and trickled a pale pink streak onto her tanned bare arm.

A crunch in the grass caught Maddy's ear, and she looked up to see David crossing the lawn. She inhaled sharply. She couldn't help admiring the slant of his shoulders and his easy, springy stride. Talking by the shower had been a disaster, but this was it. She could do it. She tried to smooth her hair with the backs of her dirty hands. Maddy focused furiously on the beans. She sensed David approaching but didn't turn around as he sat down next to the garden plot. Neither of them said anything. Maddy finally managed to look up at him. He was sneaking a glance at her at the same time. She flashed a quick smile that probably looked more like a grimace and turned back to the stake as if picking beans was her calling in life. Was this really the same guy she had hung out with all summer? Had they really eaten ribs together in a parking lot, doubled over laughing and talking endlessly? Her heart pounding, Maddy forced herself to turn around again. She knelt next to the basket and concentrated on picking out leaves.

"So, how's the garden doing?" David said.

"Great!" It came out a little loud.

"I love it that it never rains in the summer here," he said. Wow, they were talking about the *weather*? *What the hell?*

"Me too," Maddy agreed. She felt a zing like a mini electric shock as their eyes met. She swallowed hard. She'd never had to search for things to say to David before all of this. They just talked naturally, without thinking. "So . . . are you glad summer's almost over?"

He shrugged, a gesture Maddy found unbearably cute. "Yes and no. I like it here more, but I do miss people in the city. How about you? Are you going to be glad to see . . . your friends?" She caught the tiny pause before "friends." This was her chance.

"Well, yeah. I'll be glad to see Morgan and Kirsten, but . . . um . . . Brian and I broke up." She stopped fiddling with the beans and looked right at him. His mouth opened and shut twice before he found his voice.

"Wow. I had no idea."

"Yeah. It just wasn't working out. I think we were just growing apart," she said cautiously. Her heart was pounding so hard she could hear the blood in her ears. David scooted closer on the grass and brushed some dirt off of her nose.

"Hey, you know something? Earlier, when I ran into you by the shower, I really was looking for a bucket. But I was also trying to find *you*."

Maddy raised her head and met David's eyes for the first time all day. She took a deep breath. "By the way," she said, "I was thinking . . . you know, after that eggplant dish . . ." He gave a fake shudder and she smiled ruefully. "Maybe I could use a few cooking lessons . . . ?" She faltered, but a grin danced on his lips.

"Tomorrow night. Eight o'clock. Come over to the cottage. After an hour with me, I promise you'll never make Eggplant Surprise again."

Chapter Twenty-five

✦

David!" Maddy called, running breathlessly up the path to the little white cottage. Her long hair was slipping out of its ponytail, and she was wearing an old pair of gray gym shorts and a pink camisole—the first things her hand had touched when her cell phone woke her up half an hour earlier. "David!" she yelled again, trying not to slip on the gravel in her Havaianas. All of a sudden, she stopped, remembering Fred. He might not appreciate being woken up at seven o'clock, she thought, looking around quickly. His gray pickup was gone. He must already be out. *"David!"* she hollered with renewed vigor, cupping her hands around her mouth.

An upstairs bedroom window flew open and a sleep-tousled head poked out. "Are you nuts, woman?" David demanded.

"The furniture place called a few minutes ago," Maddy said from the driveway. "They're coming to deliver everything in an hour. And Standish is bringing all the wineglasses this morning too!" As soon as she had gotten the news, Maddy had called the rug dealer. She had promised that her son would be over with the rug in a couple hours. Maddy was saving that as a surprise.

David started to draw his head back in. "Just let me get dressed."

"No, wait! We left all that painting stuff in there— remember? And I think we should mop the floors and wipe everything off before they move stuff in. So come on!"

"You have way too much energy for this early," David groaned. "Okay, just wait for me while I take a shower and get something to eat. The front door's open." He disappeared.

Maddy pushed open the old screen door and stepped into a small living room. The furnishings were spartan but neat; a plaid sofa with an afghan folded across the top, a matching armchair, a couple of bookcases filled with old books. A grandfather clock ticked solemnly in the corner. Maddy wandered into the kitchen. She could hear water running upstairs. She gazed at the white stove with its gas burners, and the old fridge humming in the corner. She glanced at the clock on the stove. David would have to hurry if they were going to beat the deliverymen.

Suddenly, a thought occurred to her. This was her second chance. Excitedly, Maddy yanked open the fridge door and pulled out a carton of eggs and a half-full gallon of milk. She opened cabinet doors until she found a bowl, a whisk, and a frying pan. Quickly, she whipped three eggs and a little milk into a deep yellow froth and lit the burner. It felt good to be in control again after the trauma of her last cooking experience. She cut two thick slices off a loaf of bread on the counter and dropped them into the toaster.

She was stirring the eggs in the pan as David's footsteps sounded on the stairs. "Hey," he said suspiciously. "What's going on here?"

Maddy turned around, smiling. His normally curly hair was gleaming wet and still flat against his head. He was wearing a T-shirt that read DEADMAN TRAIL 15K and carrying his Tevas in one hand. He dropped the shoes on the floor and came over to her. Maddy's palms immediately started sweating. She grinned and held out the pan. "Breakfast?" she asked, trying to sound smooth and failing miserably. The toaster pinged.

"Wow, I'm impressed," David said, sitting down at the table. "I love a girl who makes me breakfast."

Maddy giggled—*like an idiot*, she thought—and scraped

the eggs onto a plate, adding the toast on the side. *Please try to act intelligent, Maddy,* she begged herself. It was hard, when he was so unbelievably cute.

David inhaled the eggs in four bites, piling them on top of the toast and stuffing them into his mouth. "Mmm. These are great, Mad," he said with his mouth full. Maddy beamed. He scraped up the last bits with his fork and pushed back from the table. "Okay, let's get out of here." He turned and smiled at her as if they were beginning an adventure.

Side by side, they hurried through Jenkins's field, following the path along the stream until they reached the tasting room. Maddy pushed the big double doors open and together they quickly cleared the room of the remaining painting supplies: a big blue tarp, a ladder, some paintbrushes in a bucket of water, a pile of rags. David grabbed a bottle of Windex and some paper towels and went over to the windows while Maddy mopped the floor industriously. They were almost done when Maddy heard a diesel engine rumbling from the direction of the house and a screech of brakes. Her eyes met David's.

"The stuff's here!" Maddy squealed. She had to restrain herself from jumping up and down and clapping her hands.

David dumped all the cleaning supplies into a garbage bag to take back to the house. He placed it outside the door and then turned back to Maddy, who was still standing in the middle of the floor. "Come on, Maddy-Mae, let's go meet them."

But Maddy didn't move. She was gazing around the empty space, looking at the gleaming, polished wood floor, the glistening fresh paint, the sparkling windows with the wavy glass throwing little splashes of color all over the walls. David walked over to her. "What is it?" he said, touching her shoulder. She looked up at him.

"I was just thinking of the way this place looked the first day we saw it. Remember?"

He laughed. "Yeah, I do. How could I forget? I had no idea what to make of you. But I could hardly take my eyes off you."

Maddy blushed and looked down. "I can't believe how different it looks—we've done so much this summer," she murmured.

"Well, I don't know about you," David said, looking down at her, "but this has definitely been one of the most *interesting* summers of my life."

Maddy lifted her chin. "Yeah," she said. "Me too."

The moment was broken by an engine rumble. Maddy ran to the door. A guy with a clipboard jumped down from a truck parked just outside. "Madeline Sinclaire?" he asked, consulting a sheaf of papers.

"Yes, that's me."

"Okay, I've got a delivery of furniture here. You want to tell the crew where you want things?"

He had barely finished speaking when another, smaller truck arrived with STANDISH & SONS painted on the side. The next hour was a blur of workmen in heavy boots, boxes and crates with their lids pried open, piles of packing paper and straw littering the floor, furniture emerging from its wrappings and filling the room. Little by little, stacks of glittering glassware appeared from mountains of cotton padding, covering the long oak table pushed against one wall.

Everything was almost unpacked when Maddy heard a voice by the door. She looked up. A guy about her age was squinting at a piece of paper. "Excuse me, are you Madeline Sinclaire? I have your rug here."

David looked up from where he was cramming packing paper into a box. "So that's what you were getting in town, sneaky girl!" he said, straightening up.

Maddy grinned at him. "Wait till you see it." She motioned to the guy. "Can you just prop it over there? We'll unroll it later."

The guy shrugged. "Sure," he said and manhandled the heavy column wrapped in brown paper against one wall.

At last, the workmen were gone, stuffing the wrappings and boxes into their trucks and bumping back up the path toward the house and the road. The silence felt good. Maddy took a deep breath and turned to David. "Want to see the rug now?" she asked.

"Of course. It better be pretty amazing after all this buildup," he teased. Together they stripped off the paper wrapping and, with a flourish, unfurled the rug on the shiny brown floorboards. David stepped back, his hands on his hips, and gave a low whistle. Maddy waited. She was surprised to find herself a little breathless with anticipation. "Wow," he finally said. "I'm speechless." He bent to examine the rug more closely. "This is one of the coolest things I've ever seen. How did you even know it would be so perfect in here?"

Maddy beamed. "Thanks." She walked over to stand next to David in the doorway, and together they gazed at the results of an entire summer of work. The whole place looked utterly fantastic. Two plump sofas covered in tan silk stood in opposite corners, with matching armchairs pulled up near them. Rectangular coffee tables in light maple were positioned at the perfect angle for resting glasses or propping feet. Near the middle of the room, four round bistro tables stood surrounded by elegant little straight chairs. The long oak table dominated one entire wall, crystal wineglasses lined up in perfect rows on its surface, looking just as Maddy had pictured them when she saw the table at the store.

The pure Napa light poured from the clean windows, highlighting the mellow patina of the floorboards, the crisper, sleeker wood of the tables and chairs, and the rich texture of the rug. Framed by the big open double doors was that stunning view of the mountain that Dad had shown them the very first day.

David's voice broke the silence. "Well, Mads, this room is really incredible."

"I agree," Maddy said, smiling.

"But I have to say that what really makes it stand out is that." He pointed to the rug. "It's, it's . . ." He struggled to find words in an unfamiliar vocabulary. "It's the perfect combination of rustic beauty and modern elegance!" He looked very proud of himself.

"How about the perfect combination of old and new?" Maddy suggested.

"Yeah, that's what I meant. Actually, it's the perfect combination of Napa and Maddy." Maddy looked up at him in surprise and delight. He wrapped his arms around her shoulders and pulled her against his chest. It was the closest they'd been, Maddy realized, since that day in the lake. He felt just as good now as he did then; better in fact. His warm arms felt so safe around her, she never wanted him to let go. He must have felt the same way, because he squeezed her a little tighter before finally stepping back. They were both smiling a little self-consciously, but this time Maddy didn't look away.

Chapter Twenty-six

◆

Maddy collapsed onto her bed and stared up at the ceiling after she'd confirmed that night's cooking lesson with David. Who would've thought this was how her summer would end up? She rolled over onto her stomach and remembered how David's arms felt around her. Just then, her BlackBerry on the bedside table rang. Maddy picked it up and looked at the screen. Morgan.

"Hey, babe!" she said.

"Hi!" her friend squealed. "How's everything going?"

Maddy smiled dreamily at the ceiling. "Awesome, actually."

"Wow. Um, didn't you just break up with Brian?" Morgan paused. "*And* NOT tell me or Kirsten?"

There was a moment of pregnant silence. Morgan was completely right, of course. The truth was, Maddy had been a little scared of how her friends would react. Why would anyone break up with Brian Kilburn, the sexiest guy they knew? Maddy realized she had done a lot of new things this summer. "Mor, you're right. I should have called. It's just . . . well, everything's been a little crazy."

"Okay. I'll forgive you *if* you tell me what happened with you two. We're dying to know."

Maddy rose restlessly from the bed and wandered over to the porch. She gazed out at the Napa afternoon bathed in a rich yellow glow of sun. "We were just growing apart. I mean, he came up here to visit and it was really weird. It wasn't fun at all. I felt like I couldn't talk to him anymore." She stopped and took a deep breath. "And there's something else. . . ."

Morgan screamed right in Maddy's ear. "Stop right there! I knew it. You hooked up with that guy David, didn't you?"

"No!" Maddy said, a little more emphatically than she meant to. "I mean, not really. We haven't hooked up . . . yet." She couldn't help smiling to herself a little. "But we have been hanging out a lot—and Mor, he's really cool."

Morgan sighed. "Well, obviously you're going to hook up. I'm so jealous. I haven't made out with anyone since your party, practically. It's so great to have a fling at the end of the summer. Too bad you have to leave him in a few days!"

For a minute, Maddy didn't understand what her friend meant. "Well, I might not have to. He goes to Westside Public. And Mor, I have to tell you—I think this thing between us is more than a fling. I mean . . . I really like him. I want to keep seeing him once we're both back in the city."

"What?" Morgan said incredulously.

"I . . . I think we might try this thing out—being together back home." Maddy faltered a little. She heard Morgan inhale sharply.

"Maddy. I love you, and as one of your best friends, I have to tell you when I feel like you're about to do something stupid. And this is really, really stupid!"

Maddy didn't respond.

"Look, you've spent the whole summer mucking out stalls or whatever you've been doing, and you and that guy have been all alone up there, so it's natural something would've happened with you guys."

"Well, yeah, but it's been more than that—"

Morgan let out an annoyed-sounding sigh. "Look, let me lay it out for you. Whatever it's been, you're coming back to the city now. You have a whole life here. How do you know a guy you met in Napa would fit in with us? I mean, what would you guys *do* together?"

"I don't really know . . . ," Maddy said slowly. It was true that Napa wasn't like the rest of the world—the ordinary rules didn't really apply. She felt so close to David now, but could they maintain that when they weren't in Napa? They were from very different worlds. Her head was starting to pound. "Mor, I have the worst headache. I'm going to get off and find some Advil."

"Wait! I totally forgot the whole reason I called!"

Maddy groaned. "You mean it wasn't to tell me that I was making all the wrong decisions?"

"No, but I'm glad I did. I'm having a party at Tangerine for my birthday on Wednesday and you have to come. I can't celebrate without you!"

"And I can't let you celebrate without me! But we're not supposed to get back from Napa until Thursday," Maddy told her.

"Beg! Maybe they'll let you come home early," Morgan insisted.

"Maybe," Maddy said without much hope. "They've mellowed out a lot since we left. I'll have to get them at the right moment."

"Well, at least try, okay?"

"Okay. Bye, babe."

"Bye." Morgan hung up.

Maddy dropped the phone on the floor and closed her eyes just for a second, the warm afternoon sun streaming from the balcony doors onto her face. David's image floated in front of her. They were standing in the tasting room again. He had his arms around her, but this time he was kissing her. His lips were warm and delicious. Maddy felt herself relax, the stress of the conversation with Morgan floating away. She and David were walking through the grapevines. She could feel his strong hands on her waist. . . .

Chapter Twenty-seven

✦

The radio in the kitchen was on when Maddy knocked softly at the porch door of the cottage. She hadn't been able to decide between the ultra-casual faded jeans and a white gathered eyelet tank top or the more flirty pink jersey sundress. She'd gone with the jeans in the end. David had seen her at her worst; self-consciousness was out the window.

"Come in," she heard David call. Sufjan Stevens provided the background music as she opened the screen door. The little kitchen with its neat wood cabinets and long marble countertops smelled like warm chocolate. David, wearing an army green T-shirt and jeans, stood at the counter, mixing something in a bowl, a striped dish-towel flung over his shoulder. He looked incredibly sexy. He glanced up as she entered, his hair falling in his eyes a little, and grinned at her.

Maddy held out a tub of strawberries. "I thought maybe we could use these." The little red heart-shaped berries looked gorgeous. "I picked them up at the farm stand."

"Well, well, maybe you're not a hopeless cook after all," he teased. He motioned her over to stand next to him and examined the berries while she examined him. She stared at the muscles in his arms as he dumped the berries into a colander and ran water over them. "So, we're making chocolate mousse cake," he explained. "Strawberries will go great with that."

"That sounds so good. . . ." She laughed, inhaling another strong whiff of warm, rich chocolate.

"It is—the chef at Mondavi used to tell me that he would serve this when . . ." He stopped and smiled mischievously. "Let's just say this was a dish to impress the ladies."

She laughed. "I'm impressed."

"Come here—I'll show you how to mix this," he offered.

"Okay." She stood close to him at the counter, watching as he poured a stream of melted chocolate from a small saucepan into a bowl of smooth, shiny batter. His strong arm blended the chocolate in streaks.

"See, you want to sort of fold it in very gently in kind

of an oval shape, instead of mixing around and around."
He glanced at her and smiled. "You want to try?"

"Sure." She took the spatula and tried to imitate him.

"Here, try it like this," he said after a minute, and she
felt his hand close around hers. He moved so that he was
standing just behind her.

"Like this?" she said, though she wasn't paying the
slightest attention to the batter.

"Mmhm," he said. He sounded like he wasn't paying
attention to the batter either. She leaned back into him
just the slightest bit, still folding the batter, though by
this time the chocolate had long since disappeared. She
could feel him inhale at her touch, and the muscles in
his chest tensed a little.

Ping-ping-ping! The timer on the stove sounded. He
exhaled and stepped away from her over to the stove.
"The layers are ready." The scent of cake filled the
kitchen as he pulled a pan out of the oven. Maddy wandered over to the refrigerator and peered at some photos
stuck there with magnets. She squinted at one of two tall
guys with their arms around each other's shoulders,
standing in the sun at the top of some mountain.

"Is that you?" she asked.

He turned around to see what she was looking at.
"Yeah. That's my buddy Jim. We hiked to the top of
Bismark Peak in Utah last summer." Something started
bubbling in a copper saucepan on the stove and David

quickly bent over to reduce the flame. Maddy eyed his turned back. The temptation was just too great. She plucked a berry out of the colander, took aim, and pitched it at him. It bounced off his head and fell to the floor.

"Hey!" He whirled around to face her, already laughing. She giggled and threw another one, this time catching him on the chest.

"Okay, I see how it is," he said. "Well then, how about this?" Before she could react, he scooped a spoonful of batter, closed one eye, and took aim, catapulting the cake across the room and catching her right in the face.

She squealed and wiped her eyes. "You jerk!" She darted across the room, scooped up her own glob of batter, and let it fly, splattering his shirt.

He dove across the kitchen table, trying to catch her, but she slipped away from his grasp and ran to the other side. They faced off, grinning, until he held up his hands. "Truce, okay? I give up."

"Okay." She relaxed and turned away before feeling something soft hit the back of her head. A strawberry fell at her feet. "Ooh! You're going down!" she yelled. In one quick movement, she grabbed the colander out of the sink and, evading his hands, dumped the entire contents on his head. Strawberries fell pattering at their feet like fat red raindrops and rolled to the far corners of the room.

Maddy stood, hanging on to the counter, trying to catch her breath from laughing so hard at the sight of David with the colander still on his head. With dignity, he removed the metal helmet and placed it on the counter. "Do you know you look like a raccoon?" he asked, pointing at the mask of shiny brown batter now beginning to dry on her face.

"I know," Maddy gasped, starting to regain control of herself. "Help."

"Here," he said, running a clean dishcloth under the faucet. He took hold of her shoulder with one hand and with the other wiped at her cheeks. Maddy stopped giggling like someone had turned off a switch. David looked down into her face, suddenly serious. She inhaled sharply. *He's going to kiss me, oh my God, he's going to kiss me.* She hoped he couldn't feel the slight trembling of her shoulders under his hands. From somewhere outside, the song of a killdeer reached her ears. But David's face filled her field of vision. He leaned down and she closed her eyes. For a brief moment, his hand tightened on her shoulder. Then she felt it drop away. Maddy opened her eyes in surprise.

David abruptly turned back to the stove. An awkward silence descended as he stirred something furiously. She was totally confused. Wasn't he going to kiss her? What happened? Did she have something in her teeth? She stared at David's back, trying to gauge his feelings from his posture. But his rounded shoulders told her nothing. They had been having such a good time. And he *was* going to kiss her. Maybe he was nervous. Maybe—she hated to think of it—he was having second thoughts about her. "Um, well, I should get back," she heard herself saying in a small voice.

He turned around with the saucepan in one hand. She was flooded with relief when she saw his face—desperate but not angry.

"Okay," he said in a croak. He cleared his throat and tried again. "See you later?"

"Definitely!" She tried to load all of her feelings into that one word. He nodded. They stared at each other for one long minute and then she made herself turn calmly and open the screen door, leaving him in the middle of the kitchen.

Chapter Twenty-eight

✦

Maddy was folding T-shirts into her blue suitcase when there was a knock at the door. "Come in," Maddy sang out. Mom had said she'd be bringing up the shoe basket from the back hall. But it wasn't Mom standing in the doorway when she turned around—it was David. She caught her breath. "Hey," she managed.

"Hey." For the first time since she'd known him, he looked awkward, like he didn't know what to do with his hands.

"I was just packing—"

He spoke at the same time. "Do you want to go—" He tried again. "Do you want to go for a drive?"

Maddy paused. She wasn't counting on anything after what happened earlier that evening. "Sure."

His face lit up. "I'll wait for you downstairs in the truck, okay?"

"Okay." He turned and left.

Maddy went over to the mirror on the wall and stared at herself. Her eyes were wide and sparkling and her cheeks were pink. All she needed was a little lip gloss. She quickly brushed her hair, letting it hang loose and shiny over her shoulders.

The cool, deep night surrounded her as she stepped out onto the front porch. The crickets were chirping in the trees, matching the rumble of the idling pickup truck. David sat in the cab, his elbow out the window, tapping his fingers on the steering wheel.

"So, are you kidnapping me?" Maddy teased as she got in.

"Definitely."

"Great." She settled next to him on the seat as he sped down the gravel driveway. Her hair blew against her face as the wind swept through the open windows. Neither of them said anything, but the silence was peaceful. The radio played softly as the truck's head-lights cut through the darkness. Maddy closed her eyes for a minute and let her head rest on the back of the seat.

After a little while, David turned off the highway and she could feel the truck bumping down a dirt road. She lifted her head and opened her eyes. "Where are we?"

Dark, impenetrable pine forest lined both sides of the narrow dirt track.

He smiled, his eyes straight ahead, his large, graceful hands resting on the steering wheel. "Just wait. Don't you recognize it yet?" The woods opened onto a little meadow, lit by the full moon. They were near the lake—their lake.

"Oh, I love this place," she said.

"Me too. We had such a good time that day, I thought we should visit it one more time before we left." He stopped the engine and reached behind him into the back of the cab, pulling out a basket.

They walked single file down the path to the sandy beach. The lake lay before them, a moonpath spread on the inky, glittering surface. The water made gentle splashing sounds as it lapped the edge of the dock.

David led the way onto the sand. As Maddy watched, he opened the basket he had been carrying and spread out a blanket and a container of something. Then he pulled out three little votive candles in glass holders and lit them carefully with a lighter from his pocket. Maddy was floored.

"This is so beautiful, David," she said. He smiled, more shyly than usual.

"Come here," he said, patting the blanket next to him. She sat, tucking her legs underneath her. He opened the container, revealing the finished chocolate mousse cake. "I thought we could try this." He cut two pieces and put them on little plates. Maddy broke off a bite with her fingers and put it in her mouth. It was dark and moist. "What do you think?" he asked.

"It's amazing, but I can't imagine that's because of me," she said.

"Well, you added a little extra spice." For a moment, they smiled at each other and then David looked away across the lake. He frowned, started to say something, and then stopped.

Maddy scooted a little closer to him on the blanket. "David?" she asked softly.

He looked back at her and took a deep breath. "I've got something to tell you and I'm going to have to get it out before I lose my nerve."

Maddy wondered if he could hear her heart pounding.

"I don't know about you, but for me, this summer has been one of the craziest, most confusing . . . and best two months of my life." Maddy nodded, and David, seeming to take that as a sign of encouragement, went on, his voice a little steadier. "And *you* are the reason for that." Maddy drew in a breath and watched his face. He was looking back across the water, his arms looped around his knees. His fingers were twined so tightly together the knuckles were white. "I know it'll be hard going back to the city. I mean, all of our friends will be around and everything, and we'll be back at school. . . ."

"It won't!" Maddy spoke for the first time since he had started talking. David looked down at her. "We could still see each other. I've had such a good time with you." She faltered and dropped her eyes to her lap. When she looked up, he was smiling.

"Maddy-Mae." The sound of his voice saying her name sent a shiver up her back. "I was so excited to meet you at the beginning of the summer. But then I messed it all up that first night. I thought you were totally superficial, but I was completely wrong. And then I pushed you too fast after your birthday. I should have realized you'd need time to sort things out. I was so mad at myself for screwing things up with you." He started fiddling with one edge of the blanket. From across the lake, a loon's lonely cry echoed. A soft night wind ruffled their hair. Maddy placed her hand over David's.

"You want to hear something funny?" she said. "After our fight in the orchard, I was so mad at *myself* for screwing things up with *you*." He looked up in surprise. Their eyes met and neither spoke for a long, excited moment.

"We've been having such a great time lately," David said. "Then, in the kitchen, I wanted to tell you how I felt, but I chickened out. I've been hoping–" He stopped and looked down at the blanket. "I can't think about anything but you."

This is the moment, she thought. "I have something to tell you, too. When we were in the kitchen?"

"Yeah?"

"I really wanted you to kiss me."

David let out his breath audibly and grinned. "Really?" He sounded hopeful and disbelieving at the same time.

"Yeah."

He looked into her eyes and lifted her chin. She took a deep breath as he tilted his head toward her and pressed his lips to hers softly. He drew his head back and looked at her face. "I've been wanting to do that for a long time."

"Me too," Maddy whispered. She leaned toward him and turned so that she could put her arms around his shoulders. His arms wrapped around her waist and they kissed again, more deeply this time. His lips were hot and insistent. She opened her mouth and lost herself in their kiss, sending jumps and shivers all through her body.

Slowly, still kissing, they slid down so that they were lying on the blanket, their bodies pressed together from shoulder to hip, their legs entwined. David kissed Maddy's neck and she closed her eyes and let her head fall back onto the blanket. He pulled her tighter against him and they lay holding each other under the stars, listening to the lapping of the water, not saying much—but then again, not much needed to be said.

Chapter Twenty-nine

✦

Maddy inhaled a deep breath of the crisp Napa air as she stepped out onto the front porch. Inside, her parents were frantically packing for their departure tomorrow, but she was leaving today. Morgan had apparently called the elder Sinclaires last night and convinced them to let her and Kirsten drive up and get Maddy. They were going to get lunch and then head down to the city for Morgan's party. Maddy was excited to see them, but it was a low-grade excitement. Mostly, she was consumed with thoughts of David. She was all tangled up this morning. Last night everything had seemed so easy. Now Morgan's words from their phone conversation were intruding on Maddy's happiness.

She sat down on the top porch step with her head on

her knees. She had a whole other life back in the city, one that didn't include David. And in truth, he really was different than anyone else she knew. Funny and goofy and smart, but different. The realization that she was a little different now too after this summer invaded her thoughts. *But I like my life at home,* Maddy argued with herself. *I don't* want *things to change.*

The question was flashing in neon lights in her mind: What would happen to them in San Francisco? Should they stay together? Did she want that? Did *he* want that? Maddy tried to imagine David hanging out in Morgan's hot tub with the usual crowd. She shifted uncomfortably on the hard wooden step. This summer had been so damn confusing from beginning to end—one thing that hadn't changed.

She looked at her watch. David would be here any minute. Maddy rehearsed several scenarios in her head. She could clutch him passionately and say, *"David, you're my true love, why did we wait so long to get together? I don't care what the world says. Let's defy them all, my darling."* That seemed a little extreme. Then there was the one where she froze into icy perfection and said with decorum, *"I wasn't myself last night. I'm sorry about that. Well, this summer was fun and it was nice getting to know you. Good-bye."* Or maybe, *"Want to go to the beach on Saturday with my friends and me?"* Or, *"You were an awesome kisser, maybe we can have a couple of booty calls this year."*

No. She knew what she had to do. She'd just tell him honestly that they clearly had a connection, but that she'd been thinking about it and didn't see how it was going to work back in the city. Their lives would never mesh.

David rounded the side of the house. Maddy's palms immediately started sweating as if someone had turned on a faucet in her hands, and she felt a silly grin spread over her face. His face bore a similarly goofy expression as he approached the porch. They looked at each other. "Hi," she croaked.

"Hi." He lowered himself next to her on the step. She could feel the warmth radiating from his body. He smelled wonderful. She resisted the urge to lean in to his shoulder, but he reached out and pulled her against him. She looked at him and he leaned forward and kissed her softly. For a moment, she pressed her lips against his in response, but then her fears came flooding back and she pulled away, shrugging his arm from her shoulder.

"What's the matter?" he asked. She looked at his open face and quailed a little.

"I don't know," she mumbled. A lie. "I'm worried."

"About what?" He reached for her again but she shifted away.

Before she could respond, Morgan's white Mercedes SUV pulled up the driveway and parked in front of the house. The doors flew open and her friends jumped out. "Hey!" Morgan shouted. "We're here!"

Automatically, Maddy rose from the porch steps and went toward them. "I can't believe you guys are actually here," she said, giving them each a hug. Her words sounded far away, like they were coming from someone else.

"Ohmygod, look at this place!" Morgan shrieked. "It's *so* adorable!" She was wearing one of her standard outfits, a tiny miniskirt and white tube top, with platform espadrilles that tied halfway up her legs.

Kirsten was more subdued in a gray polo-shirt dress and flip-flops. She hugged her friend again. "So, it's actually a vineyard," she said. "We were sure you'd been lying to us and you were living with Justin Timberlake up here."

Maddy's mind was still a fog but luckily the auto-response function took over. "Yeah, I am—how'd you guess? I'm keeping him down by the stream in the tasting room. I missed you girls like crazy!"

"We missed you, too!" Morgan said. "You look awesome—you're so tan!"

"Thanks. That's one thing a summer of manual labor will get you." Suddenly, she remembered David, who was standing patiently by her side. "Girls, remember the, um, guy I told you about?"

"Hey." He stuck out his hand. "I'm David. You know, the um, guy?"

The girls laughed. "Hi," they said in unison.

David smiled. "Nice to finally meet you."

"You too," they said together. Then they looked at each other and laughed.

"We have to stop that," Morgan said. "So, where should we eat around here?" she asked as the group headed toward the Mercedes.

David paused and then said, "Actually, we could check out Maddy's favorite place to eat. It's not far from here." He winked at Maddy and took her hand.

Oh no, Maddy thought, her grip tightening on David's. *No, they totally wouldn't go for–*

But David was still talking ". . . barbecue shack right on the side of the road. The meat is incredible, if you girls don't mind a picnic table."

Damn it. Maddy saw Morgan glance at Kirsten hesitantly.

Kirsten shrugged. "Sure," she said. "Why not?"

"Cool," David said as they all slid into the sleek leather seats. "You should have seen this girl put away an entire rack of ribs the other day. It was really impressive."

Morgan glanced back through the seats at Maddy, who offered a sickly smile. "Nice, Mads. I had no idea you were such a carnivore."

"Heh-heh. Um, yeah, I guess I didn't know either." Maybe the barbecue shack would be closed, she thought hopefully. Then they could all find some nice little sandwich place in town. At the back of her mind, she wondered why she was being so uptight. David was right. She *did* love it. It was just that it would never have occurred to her friends to go someplace like that back home. Actually, it wouldn't have occurred to her, either.

The cooker was smoking when they pulled up in the parking lot, and the two dogs, which didn't appear to have moved an inch since their last visit, were still watching the little old guy in the stained apron with eternal hope. Several people, most of whom looked like workers from the nearby vineyards, were waiting in line. Maddy spoke up as they piled out of the car. "David, can you get the food while we stake out the picnic table?" She had to get the girls alone for a second.

David nodded agreeably. "Sure. Ribs for everyone okay?"

"Yeah," Morgan said. "I barely ate breakfast anyway. We're starved."

"Good," David said as he headed toward the cooker. The girls collapsed at the picnic table. Maddy looked back and forth between her two friends for a few moments.

"Well?" she whispered after a long pause. "What do you think?"

Kirsten nodded slowly. "Cute."

"Yeah," Morgan said. "He's really cute, Mad."

Kirsten opened her mouth to add something, but David's figure loomed over them suddenly, loaded with steaming paper plates of ribs, corn on the cob, and warm biscuits.

"Hey, look at this!" he said, plunking the food down in front of them. "The guy recognized me and jumped me to the front of the line. Plus, he threw in the biscuits for free." He sat down next to Maddy and pulled over two of the plates.

For a long moment, no one said anything. Maddy imagined that she could see the tension floating around the table like a fog. Then Morgan swallowed a bite of corn and asked, "So, what did you guys do up here for fun all summer?"

Before Maddy could say anything, David answered, "Went biking some, did some cooking, had paint fights. The usual Napa activities."

Kirsten laughed as if David was making a joke and then stopped, seeing Maddy's expression. "Oh, you were serious. Sorry. It's just that I can't imagine Maddy cooking and having paint fights."

"Well, we did," Maddy said, a trifle defensively.

"Sounds awesome," Morgan said, and laughed. Maddy couldn't tell if she was being serious or sarcastic. Probably sarcastic, she decided glumly.

Everyone ate ribs and made conversation for the next half hour. David and the girls *seemed* pretty relaxed, but

Maddy figured they were all just trying to be polite. After all, they weren't going to be rude. But Maddy imagined she could hear what Morgan and Kirsten were thinking: *How can we get out of here? What does Maddy see in this guy? Has she gone out of her mind thinking she can date him back in the city?* They were right, Maddy thought furiously, rising to stuff her plate into the metal trash can. She had briefly gone out of her mind. Now, though, she could see the situation more clearly. The sight of the three people sitting at the picnic table—David's lanky figure in an old T-shirt and worn jeans and the two hip, perfectly groomed girls next to him—made her decision for her. It was over.

Maddy marched back to the table. "Are you all ready to go?" she asked. The others looked up in surprise at her firm tone.

"Sure," David said, getting up quickly. Everyone rose and tossed their trash away, heading toward the car.

"Your stuff's all back at the house, right, Mad?" Morgan asked, starting the engine.

"Yeah, we have to go back there first," Maddy said, her eyes on David. He was lounging easily, his arm draped around the back of the seat, looking happy and satisfied after their meal.

Maddy sat stiffly and silently until they pulled up the long gravel drive. She jumped out as soon as Morgan cut the engine. "Wait here for me, girls," she said. "David will help me get my suitcase inside." She aimed a significant glance at David, who jumped up.

"Oh, yeah. I'll just give her a hand . . . ," he said. They slammed the doors and Maddy led him around to the backyard, where she stopped and turned to face him. She took a deep breath. His forehead was creased with concern. "I guess you're going to tell me what's wrong," he said.

Now that the moment was here, she just wanted to get it over with. "I'm worried about going home."

"Huh?"

Why were guys so dense? "I'm worried about you and me," she said.

He looked confused. "What do you mean? I thought we talked about all that last night."

"We talked about us for like one minute!" Her voice rose involuntarily. David looked at her carefully.

"Why are you getting angry?"

"I'm not angry!" she said angrily. "I'm just thinking about the future, which you don't seem concerned about."

He frowned. "I'm not. What's there to be concerned about? I'm crazy about you and last night was practically the best night of my life. All the rest of it is just details."

Maddy fought back tears. "Yeah, well, details can be really important! And if you don't know that, then I think we have a problem!" In the back of her mind, she realized that what she was saying didn't make a whole lot of sense, but she couldn't stop herself. "We're going back to our old lives. Everything's going to be different."

He nodded slowly, his face hardening. "Yeah, I see what you're talking about now. You're worried I wouldn't fit into your rich-kid life in the city—like your friends might wonder if I was some hippie you'd picked up by the side of the road in Napa."

"No!" Now it was her turn to reach for him. "That's not what I mean," she pleaded, snuffling a little. "I'm just confused. These last few weeks have been like some dream and now we have to wake up to our other lives. Can't you see that?" She took his long fingers in hers and held on to them. He stared at their entwined hands for a long moment and then leaned down and kissed her fingers.

Then he released her hand and stared into the vine field. "Look," he said, choosing his words carefully, "I know what I want. I'm not saying it won't be hard. It *will* be hard, but I don't care. I want you." Maddy opened her mouth as if to protest, but he held his hand up. "But."

Her breath caught in her throat.

"But I'm not the only one here. Last time I looked, I think I was only fifty percent of whatever this is. So, I can't force anything. If we want different things . . . I guess we're going to have to say good-bye." He looked unbearably sad.

Maddy's head was spinning. He made it sound so easy—like the choices were crystal clear. But in her mind, everything was muddy. "But I don't want it to end!" she cried.

"It doesn't *have* to!" David gazed into her face, but she couldn't meet his eyes. She stared at the ground and said in a low voice, "You make it sound so easy."

"Don't you see that it can be?" he insisted.

"I . . . I think it's going to be too hard," she mumbled. Even as she was saying the words, she could feel how discordantly they jangled with the emotions in her heart. But she steeled herself. Better to end it now than have it trail on miserably for months and then end. "I have to go," she whispered, not daring to look at his face. Without waiting for a response, she whirled around and ran back to the front of the house.

Chapter Thirty

◆

Tears almost blinding her, Maddy grabbed her suitcase off the front porch. Morgan and Kirsten turned toward her as she hurried over to the car. "Mads, we were just saying what a hottie that guy is!" Kirsten exclaimed as she opened the passenger door.

"Yeah," Morgan agreed enthusiastically. "Totally different look than Brian, of course, but really yummy. And sweet, too." She turned the ignition and "Promiscuous" blared from the speakers.

Maddy barely heard her friends. All she could think was, *This is it. I'm leaving David.* Like she was moving through glue, she shoved her bag into the backseat and climbed in.

"He was so sweet to get all our food. It's obvious he's

crazy about you, Maddy," Morgan said over her shoulder as she adjusted the sun visor.

"You guys are perfect together!" Kirsten declared. The words reached Maddy's ears as if through fog. She shook her head.

"I'm sorry, what did you say?" Maddy asked, leaning forward.

"I said you guys are perfect together," Kirsten repeated, rummaging in her handbag.

She might as well have been speaking Swahili. "But we're totally different! Lunch just proved it. Morgan was right. We should just forget it." Maddy slumped back against the seat and crossed her arms.

Morgan threw the car into park and turned around. She turned the music way down. "Wait, what are you talking about, 'Lunch just proved it'?"

Maddy stared at her incredulously. "Lunch was a disaster," she said, speaking very slowly and clearly. "It was the most awkward experience ever."

Morgan wrinkled up her face. "What are you talking about? Lunch wasn't awkward at all. It was really fun. He clearly knows how to have a good time."

"But—but you said it would never work out!" Maddy insisted.

"*On the phone!* I'd never even met the guy. Besides, aren't I allowed to be wrong sometimes?"

"I guess," Maddy said slowly. Morgan faced front again.

"Don't worry, Mad," she said, turning the music back up and putting the car into drive. "Let's just get started on our road trip! Woo-hoo!" She started to turn around in the driveway.

Suddenly, Maddy shouted, "Stop, Morgan!" She unbuckled her seat belt.

"What?" Morgan yelled back.

"Turn the music down! Stop!"

Morgan stepped on the brakes. "What is it?"

"I have to . . . I can't . . ." Maddy looked around wildly. "Open your sunroof!"

"Are you cracked? What are you talking about?"

"Open your sunroof!" Morgan stared at her for a second and then buzzed the roof back. Maddy stood up on the seat, stuck her head and shoulders out the window, and looked toward the house. She couldn't see the yard. Quickly, she hoisted herself out of the sunroof and onto the top of the car. She stood up carefully, her sundress hem fluttering in the breeze. Now she could see the backyard and the path running through the vines. A dark head was just visible above the grape leaves.

Maddy took a deep breath. *"David!"* she yelled. He didn't turn around. *"David!"* He saw her and stopped walking. She waved her arms. "Come here!" She could see him pause. It felt like a long time. Then he started walking back up the path toward the house again. She crouched down on the car roof and hopped onto the trunk and then to the ground. Somewhere in the background, she was aware that the music had stopped and that Morgan and Kirsten had gotten partially out of the car and were watching her with avid interest. But she couldn't think about them right now.

She ran around to the side of the house and collided full-on with David. He caught her and staggered but managed to keep his balance. He held her by the shoulders a little away from him. "What is it?" he asked. "Why were you on the car roof?"

"I . . ." Maddy panted a minute, then got her breath. "I . . ." *Say it!* "I was wondering . . . if you wanted to come back with me to San Francisco? With my friends . . . ? She faltered a minute under his piercing gaze.

"What are you saying?" His hands gripped her shoulders tighter.

She inhaled. "I'm saying I want you to come back to the city with me—I want us to go back together." Her voice was clear now and the words felt right.

His face lit up like someone had turned on a switch inside him. "Are you sure?"

She nodded. He grinned and then grabbed her, pulling her to him. She wrapped her arms around his neck and he kissed her. The sound of Morgan's horn interrupted them. They broke apart and smiled at each other. Maddy took his hand and they walked together toward the waiting car.

"Oh, no!" Maddy stopped short. "What about all of your stuff? You haven't packed or told your dad . . ."

David smiled. "Maddy, I'm a guy. 'All my stuff' barely fills one bag. And my dad was going to drive to the city with me in a few days, anyway. I'll call him from the road. Now, stop interrupting the spontaneous romance of this moment!" He kissed Maddy softly and squeezed the back of her hand as he pulled her toward her friends.

She opened the door and slid into the backseat again. This time, David slid in next to her. Two amazed faces peered around the middle of the front seats. "Girls," Maddy said, "is it okay if David comes back to the city with us?"

Morgan turned all the way around and looked right at him and then at Maddy. She studied them both for a long time and then grinned. "Definitely," she said. Kirsten nodded in agreement.

"Thanks for letting me tag along on your road trip," David told them.

"No problem," Morgan replied. "I'm glad you could come." Maddy gave her a look of thanks.

"Yeah, me too," Kirsten seconded. Maddy reached forward and squeezed both of their hands. They squeezed back.

As Morgan sped down the driveway, Maddy settled back into the seat, her thigh pressed against David's. He draped his arm around her shoulder and pulled her up against him. Outside of the window, the fields and trees flashed past and the road to the city uncurled before them. Maddy relaxed into David's side, feeling safe and purely happy. She breathed in his fresh, soapy scent and it mixed with the pine-tinted Napa air. She and David fit together—here in this car, under the majesty of a Napa sunset, and in the bustle of city life. If this was what life with David was like in a place she was supposed to hate, Maddy couldn't wait to see what the city had in store.

Julianne just met the boy of her dreams. And he just happens to be her family's only enemy.

Keep reading for a sneak peek of Hailey Abbott's
FORBIDDEN BOY

◆

"Okay, well, see you around." Julianne looked down at the ground. She could barely breathe.

"Okay. Well, I guess I'll see you." Remi's voice was barely audible, his shoulders sloping downward.

Jules felt like her heart was being ripped out of her chest, but she tossed her shoulders back, laced her fingers through her belt loops, and straightened her back as she started to walk away. Fifty yards down the beach she heard Remi's voice.

"Hey, Julianne!" Remi was suddenly right beside her again, breathing heavily after his sprint. "You forgot this." He tucked a scrap of paper into her hand. "My phone number." Not smooth—definitely not smooth—but very cute. "You know, in case your sister needs it for health insurance or whatever. And so you can give me that tour. It's hard work getting jaded on your own, you know." He grinned.

"Definitely." She smiled back. "I wouldn't want to leave you hanging."

Remi's face softened as he stared right into Julianne's eyes. She felt like he could actually see inside her head—that somehow, effortlessly, they already understood each other. Softly, he put his hand on the side of her face and Julianne felt like the spot was on fire. Julianne's heart started to race with a mix of giddiness and panic. She had just met this guy, and she was already feeling totally swept away. Was she completely crazy? Swimming inside the feeling, Julianne shut her eyes. She felt their bodies move closer to each other, and then his lips touched hers. Julianne felt like she was floating above the beach—watching the moonlight reflecting off the water, the huge expanse of perfectly flat sand, the couple on the ground kissing. It was as if fireworks were exploding everywhere. She felt like the entire beach had been electrified by their kiss.

"I'm sorry—I'm really, really sorry," Julianne murmured, breaking out of Remi's arms. "I have to go. I don't know where Chloe went and I don't know if she's okay. I need to find her." Julianne's throat was dry. It was like the very worst part of every fairy tale. Suddenly she was Cinderella at midnight. "I'll call you, I promise." She flashed the scrap of paper with a triumphant smile before taking off down the beach in search of her sister.

Julianne drifted toward the small parking lot where they'd left the car a few hours earlier. She couldn't stop thinking about the kiss. It had just felt so *meant to be* somehow. A guy she had never seen before had literally fallen right into her lap—okay, well, her sister's lap, but close enough—at the start of the summer, on the beach she loved.

And he wasn't just any guy. Julianne couldn't put her finger on it, but there was something special about Remi. As she scanned the tiny parking lot, she made a mental note to give her big sister some "I told you so" points for dragging her out to this party.

Out of the corner of her eye, Julianne saw Chloe sitting on the ground, leaning against the bumper of their car, her head resting next to a faded "Imagine Whirled Peas" bumper sticker that their dad had stuck on. Julianne crept over and put her hand on Chloe's shoulder. "Chloe," she said softly, kneeling next to her sister. "Sorry I disappeared, I was just . . . saying good-bye to someone. C'mon, let's go."

Chloe opened her eyes, and turned to face Julianne. "Tell me everything."

Steamy summer reads

Forbidden Boy

When Julianne falls for Remi at a bonfire party, it looks like her summer is off to a perfect start. Then she discovers that her awful new neighbors are Remi's parents, making him a forbidden boy. But what do you do when your worst enemy is also the boy of your dreams?

The Other Boy

When she gets caught throwing a party, Maddy's parents force her to spend the summer with them, hours away from her boyfriend. But things start looking up after she meets David. When they realize they share a passion for cooking, will love start with the very first bite?

The Perfect Boy

When AJ, a hot rapper, shows interest in Heidi instead of her, Ciara and her friend Kevin devise a plan to help her win AJ over. But the closer Ciara gets to Kevin, the more she wonders, who really is the perfect boy?

y Hailey Abbott!

Waking Up to Boys

Chelsea's more comfortable strapped onto her wakeboard than flirting with Todd, the adorable watersports instructor she's been crushing on for years. So she concentrates on winning this summer's Northwest Extreme Watersports Competition. That is, until hot, Brazilian Sebastian wakes her up to the fact that she can get a boy. But can she get the one she really wants, even if she's competing against him for the gold?

The Secrets of Boys

A California girl like Cassidy should be out on the beach with her boyfriend, not stuck in summer school! But her life heats up when she meets the worldly and romantic Zach. Will temptation be too strong to resist?

Getting Lost with Boys

When Jacob offers to drive with her to her sister's place in Northern California, Cordelia's neatly laid out summer plans quickly turn into a wild road trip, where anything can—and does—happen. Who knew getting lost with a boy could be so much fun?

Don't miss the hilarious novel
She's So Money

What happens when a good girl teams up with a total player and creates the biggest scandal their school has ever seen?

When popular guy Camden convinces Maya the only way to save her family's Thai restaurant is to do other kids' homework for cash, she soon finds out that everything has a price. Especially falling in love.

CPSIA information can be obtained at www.ICGtesting.com
Printed in the USA
LVOW08s1828220916

505316LV00003B/4/P